Bad Decisions

IVY MARIE

Ivy Marie

IVY MARIE PUBLISHING

Contents

One

ROXANNE

"HAVE A NICE DAY." I smiled as my client paid for her nails.

I love it when clients leave happy. Especially when they are new. Turning to Lexi, I leaned over the counter, feet off the ground, to look at her computer screen.

"Who's next?"

"Mrs. Ruth." She stated, not even bothering to look at the computer. "She's here for her two-week fill."

Lexi pushed at my forehead with her index finger until my feet were planted firmly on the ground. I laughed as I turned to the waiting area, taking the three strides before calling out to my next client. Mrs. Ruth, the first client at Dagger Designs, sat in the cushioned chair chatting away with another waiting client. The elderly woman smiled warmly when I called for her. She lifted her purse off her lap and followed me to my station. Once seated, she repeated what she'd like done at today's appointment, then struck up a conversation.

Mrs. Ruth is a grandmother of five granddaughters and loves to tell me stories about them. She practically vibrated as she spoke of them, proud of her grandchildren and their parents. Mrs. Ruth isn't one of those stereotypical grandmothers with grey hair who prefer to knit while sitting in front of the TV. Nope. She loves to travel and go on adventures with her family. Her hair revealed a few silver strands weaved among the brown, and she dressed to impress. The woman knows how to live her life like there's no tomorrow. That's how I'd like to be when I'm closer to her age.

Mrs. Ruth was telling me about the trip she'll be having with her eldest granddaughter this coming weekend when the door to my salon flew open. It slammed into the half wall that separated the waiting area from the entrance. The wall stopped the door from hitting a client who sat waiting for her appointment. I looked up from my work at the sudden loud noise to see three people walk in.

I frowned as I took in the two women. The third person remained partially hidden from my view. The leading woman held her head high. Her tall, thin frame, accentuated by her high heels and body-hugging clothing, screamed high maintenance. Her brown hair was draped stylishly over her shoulders, and her makeup looked movie-star perfection even from this distance. I took in the other woman. She had short, straight pink hair, and her makeup was brighter but still sleek. She was a head shorter and a few pounds heavier than the first woman, and her clothing showed off her curves proudly. I suspected they were used to getting whatever they wanted.

"Good day." Lexi greeted politely, her voice carrying across the salon.

"How can I help you?"

"This is a nail emergency!" The brunette slammed her hands down on the counter.

"I'm sorry, but all of our nail technicians are currently with clients. You're welcome to have a seat and wait for someone to become available."

"How dare you make us wait!" The pink-haired woman's voice was shriller in pitch than the brunette's.

"Would you like to make an appointment instead?"

"I need new nails." The brunette paused.

"NOW!"

"Then I suggest you find another salon to assist you better with this time-sensitive matter." Lexi responded sweetly.

I couldn't help the small smile as I continued working on Mrs. Ruth's nails. Lexi — friend and receptionist extraordinaire. She has the patience of a goddess when behind that desk. We met in college, both of us taking a business course as an elective. When I talked about opening up Dagger Designs, she excitedly wanted to join me on the business adventure as my first hire. I wanted her as a business partner, but she didn't want that role. It didn't take me long to learn that behind her façade of patience, she has no tolerance for rude, obnoxious, or demanding people. When she's behind that counter, she is nothing but professional. *Lexi can handle this.*

"Either get me your boss, or you'll have to find a new job!" The brunette threatened.

"Have a seat." Lexi told her coolly. "She's currently busy with a client."

"NOW!" The woman exclaimed.

Hell no. No one treats my staff so rudely.

That was the second outburst and the last straw. Compared to Lexi, I have zero tolerance for demanding people. I could hear murmuring from both clients and employees alike. I couldn't pick out their exact words, but I could guess what was being said. This woman's tantrum will go on no longer. Apologizing to Mrs. Ruth, I excused myself from her nearly finished nails. She waved me off, telling me to do what I must do.

Rolling the chair away from my station, I stood. I could feel the eyes on me, wanting to know how I'd handle the situation. Casually, I made my way to the front, halting at the little half-step between entry and the salon floor with my arms crossed. I sent Lexi to finish Mrs. Ruth's nails for me. All she needs is a topcoat.

I kept my gaze on the brunette. "You're being disruptive."

"Do you know who I am?" She placed long fingers lightly on her chest as if she was insulted that I didn't treat her like royalty.

Honestly, I don't care who she is. I kept my mouth shut, keeping that remark in my head. When she walked into my salon, she was just another client. Now that I was up close, a niggling sensation in the back of my mind told me that I'd seen her before, but I couldn't quite pinpoint from where.

"Princess, if you want any work done here, you'd better reset the attitude." I finally answered.

"How dare you." Her voice went up an octave, definitely insulted.

"How dare I?" I repeated, insulted myself. "You come barreling into the salon with such force that the door hit the installed safety wall. You demand service, and you yell at employees. Do you honestly expect to be served?"

"Where is your boss?" The pink-haired woman stepped forward, jabbing a finger into my shoulder. "I'll have you fired."

At that moment, my brain clicked in. I know exactly who they are. Candi, a social media influencer and her pink-haired friend Brina. They are well known for making and breaking businesses here in Frostham. If businesses don't please them, they are dissed online and lose many customers. On the flip side, if Candi and Brina rave about a company, those businesses see an influx of customers. Lately, they've been focussing on nail salons. It was only a matter of time before they reached mine.

"Reset the attitude." Pointing to the door, I continued. "Or get out of my salon."

"Your salon?" Candi let out a single bark of laughter. "So, you're the owner."

"We can ruin you." Brina added proudly.

"I'm aware of your influence, princess." I intentionally spoke directly to Candi.

Brina isn't a real threat. She is only famous because she's friends with Candi. It didn't matter who spoke the threat, though. I wanted to slap them both and kick them out of my salon. Mrs. Ruth touched my arm lightly, drawing my attention to her. During my stand-off with Candi, Lexi finished Mrs. Ruth's nails and collected the payment. She slipped past the two women and out of my salon.

"Let me rephrase my earlier statement." I repositioned my hands to my hips. "If you want your nails done in my salon, you will apologize to my staff for your outburst."

"I will do no such thing." Candi countered. She turned to the third person who came in with them. "Do you hear how she's speaking to me?"

I shifted on my feet to get a better look at the person. My breath caught. The man who leaned casually against the vertical window beam had to be pulled out of some wet fantasy. He's tall, lean, and oozing sex appeal in his tailor-made black suit. The top two buttons of his dress shirt were undone to reveal his tanned skin. Our eyes met, and a heat wave flooded my body that pooled south. His dark gaze spoke of a domineering promise that had my knees wanting to buckle under the intensity. With that one look, I knew he could give me — or any woman — the best night of their life.

The man shifted his gaze to Candi. "Apologize."

His deep, smooth voice rumbled the order. I resisted the urge to close my eyes and moan. *Damn it!* His voice alone held so much power. It took all my willpower not to melt where I stood. Candi took a tentative half-step back.

"I'm sorry." She whispered.

"Not to me." His tone darkened dangerously. "To her."

"I'm sorry." Candi turned back to me. She then turned to Lexi, who watched the interaction from behind her desk. "I'm sorry. My attitude was unbecoming."

Lexi took a moment to consider the apology, then nodded, a soft smile gracing her lips. "Apology accepted."

I held out my hands with a sigh. "Let me see this emergency."

Candi quickly placed her hands in mine. I shouldn't be indulging this princess, but I'll also accept the apology since Lexi accepted it. I scrutinized each finger. The build is too thick, the shaping is uneven, and the polish is streaky. *Why did she allow the tech to go this far?* Candi didn't have to tell me where she had her nails done. I knew based on the colour of the polish used. Only one salon in Frostham uses this specially blended shade.

For personal reasons, I decided to give Candi a new set of nails. I took a quick picture of her nails before taking her to my station. The first step is to remove the horrible build before starting this entire process from scratch. Mr. Suit pushed off the wall to hover over Candi while I shaped her newly made nails. His tall frame cast a shadow across my workstation.

I looked up at him. "Can I help you?"

"Not at this moment."

"Then either pull up a chair to watch or return to your post." I ordered, bending my head back over Candi's nails. "You're blocking my light."

The man moved around the table to stand behind me. His shadow was no longer cast across the tiny canvas, but it wasn't any better. The hairs on the back of my neck prickled at his nearness. *What is it about this man?* My body hummed with awareness. I glanced up at the sound of a vibrating phone. It wasn't Candi's or Brina's. The man behind me made an unimpressed sound, not quite a grunt, but similar. Or, maybe it was more like a tsk. In my periphery, I saw him bend down to kiss Candi on the cheek, and then he left the salon. It wasn't much longer after that that I had Candi's nails painted a single sparkling teal shade. Once complete, she scrutinized the work.

"One colour, how dull." Candi stated. "It'll do. Let's go, Brina."

"Not before you pay, princess." I told them.

"Why should we pay?" Brina countered with a sneer. "You saw the state of Candi's nails."

"This is a business, not a charity. If you wanted free work, you should have had the salon that screwed up fix the error." I explained tersely.

"Why would we ever let them touch our nails again?"

Candi held up her hand to stop her friend. "How much?"

"Because I'm a nice person, I'll give you this one-time-only deal. I won't charge you for the removal, but you have to pay for the new set." I walked them over to Lexi, telling her how to charge them. "If you ever return to my salon, princess, I expect a better attitude."

Candi's lips thinned, but she nodded her agreement. Part of me hoped she wouldn't return, but another part knows it'll be good for business if she does. Once they were gone, I bent over the receptionist counter, my arms stretched across its surface and laid my head down.

"They were a handful." Lexi stated softly with an exasperated sigh.

"Mrs. Ruth was supposed to be my last client." I turned my head to see her.

"You're done now." She leaned forward on her forearms, a knowing smile on her pink lips. "Mr. Suit was easy on the eyes."

I smiled at her. "I wouldn't mind him returning."

She laughed, agreeing with me. "Do you want me to call Carole?"

"No. I'll pay her a surprise visit."

"Okay. I'll see you tomorrow, Rox."

I cleaned and sanitized my workstation before returning to my office to grab my purse. I wanted to stop at Carole's before heading to my parent's house for supper tonight. I took the back door to the private parking for staff members and slipped into my car. Weaving through the streets of Frostham, I made my way to Nails R Us, located in a strip mall about twenty minutes away from my salon.

I went to high school with Carole. We had a frenemies type of relationship. We constantly fought and tried to one-up another while supporting each other when bullies got in our way. I'd never admit to Carole that our little competitive rivalry was one of the reasons why high school was so much fun.

Carole had opened her salon a few short months after I did. Our little high school rivalry continuing. The receptionist recognized me and informed me that Carole was in her office but may be busy. I made my way to the back. Voices could be heard from the open doorway — Carole's and a man's. I stopped at the door and stared. *What is he doing here?*

Two

NICO

I met up with my sister for lunch and couldn't stop staring at her hands. Well, her nails, more precisely. They were monstrous. They were utterly misshapen and disgusting. *Cristo. How could she let someone do this to her?*

"Nico, will you come with me?" Candi questioned, jutting her lower lip in a pout.

"Where?" I responded cautiously.

"To a salon."

"There's this place called Dagger Designs." Brina, Candi's best friend, began. "They are supposed to be really good."

"Why do I have to go?" I asked.

"Moral support."

"Please, Nico." Candi pleaded.

I stared at my sister. I want to say no, and I should say no. With a reluctant sigh, I agree. It'll just be a couple more hours away from work. With a pleased smile, she jumped into a new topic with Brina. I tuned them out. A skill I've acquired since the two of them became friends.

Dagger Designs didn't look unique on the outside or the inside. True to Candi fashion, if she wants something her way, she'll throw a fit to get it. My sister demanded loudly and petulantly for a new set of nails to be done. I shook my head subtly, wondering why she bothered to drag me here. I blame our parents for her attitude. Our mother gave her everything she could ever want, and when she passed, Candi quickly learned that she could continue to get what she wanted by throwing a tantrum. Our father just wanted her quiet and out of sight, so he'd give into her demands. I tried to keep her safe from the darkness in our family and provided her with whatever she asked for to keep her out of trouble. Maybe I'm to blame too.

"Princess, if you want any work done here, you'd better reset the attitude."

My ears perked up at the irritated voice. I'm used to my sister's tantrums that I subconsciously tune out. This was the first time in a long time that someone was standing up to my sister. *This should be interesting.* Sure enough, my sister didn't disappoint. She shot back at the person, insulted, and even Brina added a threat. This didn't throw that sweet-sounding voice off her game. Candi turned to me expectantly.

The woman she was arguing with peered around Candi to look at me. Not only did her eyes widen, but I saw her breath catch, too. The feeling was mutual. The honey-blonde woman with hazel eyes stole my breath away. Candi blocked my entire view of the woman's body, but those eyes of hers had me paying attention. Full attention.

There was a clear interest in her gaze as she looked me up and down. It heated my skin. Intrigued, I decided to take her side in this painfully annoying argument and had Candi apologize. She reluctantly accepted the apology before her focus became my sisters' nails. She turned to head back to a table, and I got a brief view of her ass in those jeans of hers. *Cristo.*

No woman has been able to catch my interest in nearly six years. Sure, I've taken quite a few to bed, but I don't remember their names and never cared for a second encounter. A man has needs, after all. Needing to redirect my focus, I pulled out my phone. Finding out who botched Candi's nails should be an adequate distraction. I tracked down the area where Candi last used her credit card and texted a friend to hack into nearby cameras to find the exact salon she went to. I could have done a map view of the area myself, but this option let me examine the woman working with some small machine to remove the lousy nail job. At some point, I found myself drifting over to her.

"Can I help you?" She looked up at me with a raised brow.

"Not at this moment."

"Then either pull up a chair to watch or return to your post." She ordered. "You're blocking my light."

I bit back a laugh. *Feisty woman.* Moving behind her, I noticed the slight tensing of her shoulders and the subtle floral scent coming from her. If my phone hadn't vibrated, I might have found myself leaning in closer for a better whiff of her scent.

The text had my answer: Nails R Us. I left Candi and Brina to track down this salon. It was about twenty minutes away in a strip mall. *Candi got her nails done here?* It looked just like all the other nail salons in Frostham. When I demanded to see the owner, the receptionist fearfully pointed to the back. Good. I wouldn't want someone to think that this is a social call.

"Who are you?" Green eyes glared up at me when I entered the back office.

"We need to talk." I announced.

"Who are you?" She repeated.

I scanned her face. There was a mole under her left eye, the only thing that seemed to stay in place as this brunette scowled at me. She was putting up a decent act of bravery, but her eyes showed a hint of fear. *We'll see how long that bravery of yours will last.* I kept my face neutral and my tone calm but menacing as I strolled closer, purposefully moving with calculated, intimidating steps.

"My sister came here earlier today to have her nails done." I scowled at the memory. "And someone royally fucked up."

"I'm sorry to hear that. Why are you here?"

"I want to have a chat with that person." I tried to say it pleasantly, but the disgust at the horrid workmanship coated my words.

"Do you know the name of the tech who did the work?"

I ground my teeth. "No."

"Then I'm afraid I can't help you." Her spine straightened.

"Like hell, you can't." I moved around the desk. Spinning her chair to face me, I leaned forward, resting my hands on the arms. "If you want to be able to open this place up tomorrow, you'll get me that name."

"I don't appreciate being threatened." Her glare intensified.

"It's not a threat. It's a promise."

"Leave." Her tone hardened. "Or else I'll call the police. I already said I can't help you."

I was mildly impressed that this woman wasn't cowering. A knock drew both of our attention to the door. There stood the woman from the other salon. *What is she doing here?*

A single elegant brow rose. "Am I interrupting?"

"Roxanne." The woman in the chair frowned. "What an unwanted surprise."

The woman looked over at me as she strode into the office. It was a quick glance, enough to say she noticed me but otherwise didn't acknowledge my presence. For some reason, that irritated me. While she returned her focus to the woman in the chair, I kept my eyes on her.

She entered the office with a smile and stopped on the other side of the desk. "Can't I just stop by?"

"You want something."

"Information." Roxanne stated.

"What kind of information?" The brunette asked hesitantly.

The exchange was awkward. I still leaned on the chair arms, crowding this woman's space while both of our heads were turned toward Roxanne. Both women were completely ignoring me.

Roxanne pulled out her phone, looking for something. "I want to know who did these nails."

The woman in the chair didn't move to take the phone, which showed a picture of my sister's nails. She glanced at it, but there was no way she could truly see what was on the tiny screen. I snatched the phone from Roxanne and shoved it in the woman's face with a growl. She will look at the picture and tell me who ruined my sister's nails.

"Answer her." I said through clenched teeth.

She glared at the picture and then turned that glare onto Roxanne. "Call off your enforcer."

"Enforcer?" I echoed, both insulted and amused.

Roxanne laughed. I pushed off the chair. Crossing my arms, I glared at the honey-blonde woman. No one has ever dared to laugh at me.

"What is so funny?" I demanded. My voice was intentionally low and menacing.

She waved a hand in front of her face and completely ignored me. "Carole. Why would I ever spend money on an enforcer?"

She took the phone from my hand and shoved me away. I stumbled back a step enough to allow her to stand in front of this Carole woman. Again, the image was shown to Carole.

"Who did these nails?" Roxanne asked again, emphasizing each word.

Carole took a good look at the picture. "None of my techs did this."

"Liar." I growled, leaning in again. "My sister was here. Someone in this salon butchered her nails."

"Back off, enforcer." Roxanne put a hand on my chest, pushing me back. "You're not needed."

Not needed? My mind whirled at her statement. No woman has ever said I wasn't needed. A sudden urge to make her need me sprang forth. Now is not the time or place. A knock drew all of our attention to the door. A girl with blue-tipped hair looked upon the scene with wide eyes.

"Aunt Carole, is everything okay here?" The girl's gaze flicked nervously to me.

"Just fine, sweetie." Carole offered the girl a kind smile, but I noticed her body stiffen slightly at the sight of her. "Head on home. I'll see you in the morning."

"Good night, Aunt Carole. Good night, Roxanne."

"Good night." Both women chimed.

Roxanne waited for the girl to be out of sight before clicking her tongue. "This isn't the first time Carole."

"I'm handling it Roxanne."

"Not well enough, obviously. I'll handle it this time."

"You can't." Carole exclaimed, jumping to her feet.

"I will." She turned, walking toward the door. "You have two days, Carole. Come, enforcer, there's nothing more for us to do here."

I didn't follow right away. Mostly because I didn't know what the fuck just happened. Roxanne was out the door by the time I moved to follow her. Not without shooting Carole one final glare. Roxanne was nearly to her car when I caught up with her outside.

"I am not an enforcer." I growled.

"You're not?" She questioned playfully, unlocking her car. "You certainly look like one."

"No." I closed the car door she had started to open. "I am not Roxanne."

She tried opening the door again, but I held it firmly shut. "Do you mind?"

"I want to hear you say it."

With a sigh, she turned to face me. Leaning back against her car, she crossed her arms under her breasts. My eyes were drawn to the action. I stared at the creamy mounds she pushed upward, a hint of pink from the edge cup of her bra barely visible. *Fuck I want to touch them.* With a strained moan, I forced my eyes back to her face. The woman's seductively plump lips curved upward into a smile, and her beautiful hazel eyes glinted with mischief. She knew I'd look, knew it would distract me.

I scowled at her, refusing to let her distraction plan succeed. "I'm waiting."

Her smile faltered slightly. "You're not an enforcer. Happy?"

"Not quite." I leaned in closer.

This teasing game works both ways.

"What will it take for you to let me leave?" She questioned. "I'm late for dinner."

It better not be dinner with another man. I want this woman. If there's another man in her life, he will have to go.

18

"I'll start with your name."

"You already know my name." She countered.

"Then your last name." I smiled politely. "My name is Nico Frangione."

Her eyes searched mine, debating. "Roxanne Baxter."

I know that name, but how? "It's a pleasure to meet you — officially — Roxanne."

"Now, can I please leave?"

"Of course." My hand slid down to the door handle and opened the car door for her. Roxanne slid into the driver's seat. "Have a safe drive Roxanne. I'll see you later."

I closed the door on her and let her drive off. I watched the taillights recede in the distance before heading to my car. Roxanne is a fascinating woman, and I want to learn more about her. Her name, though, bothered me. I racked my brain during the drive to my condo building, trying to remember where I'd heard it before. Just as I parked in the underground parking lot, it hit me.

Please be wrong. I repeated the mantra in my head up to my penthouse on the top floor. The elevator didn't move as fast as I needed it to go. Thirty-three-floors later, the doors finally opened. Once inside, I pulled out my laptop and searched for the email where I thought the Baxter name had been mentioned.

"Fottermi!"

I stared at a picture of Roxanne, her parents, and her brother. A few months ago, my father sent this picture to the family with a warning about Captain Baxter's investigation into the Frangione's business. I shouldn't be anywhere near this woman. Her brother, also a cop, is bound to be involved in the investigation, too.

I couldn't pull my eyes away from the image of Roxanne's laughing face in the candid photograph. Now that I've interacted with her, there's no way I cannot see her again.

For two years, I've been trying desperately to keep clean and separate myself from the Frangione business. The name and what they do in the shadows are nothing I want to be involved in. It's also probably the reason why the cops have been tailing me the past month, or at least have been trying to. I've gotten pretty good at losing the tail, but eventually, they find me again. Compared to my brother and father, I'm an easy target.

Maybe Roxanne is precisely what I need to separate myself from the Frangione family business completely. Prove to my father that I'm serious about cutting ties. It'll be dangerous. No one has ever left the family business before. That I know of. I do know that I don't want to go to jail just because I'm my father's son. He may be a criminal, but I'm not.

Roxanne will be the key to staying out of jail. I'll have to be careful not to be caught by my father. Knowing him, he'll use Roxanne as leverage against her father. It could be too risky to bring her into this.

I continued to stare at Roxanne's picture. I remembered the swell of her breasts, the bite to her words, and that mischievous glint in her eyes. My cock hardened at the idea of having Roxanne in my bed. *Fuck the consequences.*

"Roxanne Baxter, be ready to be swept off your feet."

Three

ROXANNE

DAHLIA STORMED INTO MY office the day after the confrontation I had with Carole. She slammed her hands on my desk childishly to get my attention. Very slowly, I looked away from my computer. The teenager glared at me.

"Why am I here?" Dahlia sneered.

I raised a single brow. She was throwing a fit. I gestured to a seat. Dahlia clenched her hands into fists. With a huff, she let her backpack fall off her shoulder, sat heavily in the chair, and crossed her arms. Lacing my fingers together, I gave the teenager my full attention.

"Why am I here?" She repeated.

"That's an excellent question." I prompted calmly. "Why are you here?"

She mumbled something I couldn't quite hear.

"Care to repeat that a little louder, Dahlia? It seems my maturity couldn't quite pick up what you've said." I taunted.

"Aunt Carole said she couldn't protect me this time, and I had to be here."

I suspected that's not what she had mumbled. I let it slide. This little tantrum reminds me of Carole back in high school. She'd throw a fit when I beat her in the mini art competitions that our school hosted to showcase their student's work.

"You've been working for your aunt for what? Two years now? I know she's been teaching you how to build nails." I explained while unplugging my phone from the charging cord in my computer. "When you first started, she bragged about how fast you picked up the trade."

"I've only gotten better over the years."

"Have you now?" I queried doubtfully, pulling up the image of Candi's nails. "These are from a recent client."

"So?" She leaned forward to see the image.

"I'm sure you recognize them."

Dahlia leaned back in the chair. "That woman deserved what she got. She was talking crap about Aunt Carole's salon."

"All the more reason to have given her the best nails ever." Leaving the phone open on the desk near her, I stood, headed over to the filing cabinet and pulled out the file I'd prepared earlier that morning. "Come with me."

"What? Why would I do that?" Dahlia grabbed her bag as she scrambled to follow anyway. "Roxanne."

"Keep up, Dahlia. I have a challenge for you." I led her out onto the salon floor to where a station was set up with

23

building supplies and dummy practice hands. "Show me your skills. I want to see gel and acrylic applications for short and long nails. Each finger should be a different shape: rounded, almond, stiletto, square, and coffin."

Dahlia crossed her arms with a snort and a roll of her eyes. "I don't need to show you anything."

"Then I guess you don't want to get into Clavus Schola."

"Clavus Schola?" She repeated, eyes widening. "You mean the best nail school in Frostham?"

"The one and only."

"Application closes this Saturday."

I handed her the file I'd brought with me. "I need this application returned by Friday."

Hesitantly, she took the file and opened it to see the application form. "But I can't afford the fee."

"Prove that you understand basic nail building, and I'll invest in your future."

"Why?"

I smiled softly at her. "Carole has shown me your art. You have the potential to be great, Dahlia, but only if you're willing to put in the effort."

Determination set on Dahlia's features. *That's what I want to see.* Slipping the file into her backpack, she sat and began to work. I left her to concentrate. I intended to chat with some clients, but Lexi caught my eye. She cocked a brow, and I knew I couldn't ignore her silent question. I made my way over, joining her behind the reception counter. I rested my hip against the side and faced her. Lexi spun on the high back stool.

"Spill." She ordered.

"Spill what?" I inquired innocently.

"What is Carole's niece doing here?"

"It all started with a mild threat." I waved a hand casually in front of my face. "Carole's been bragging about Dahlia for years, and I've seen her impressive artwork. I want the girl to work here."

"So, you're training her?"

"Nope." I grinned. "I'm going to send her to Clavus Schola."

Lexi let out a low whistle. "Does Carole know?"

"Absolutely not."

"She won't be happy about you going behind her back like this."

I laughed lightly. *Of course not.* I grinned, imagining Carole's face when she learns that I was poaching her niece.

"I live for pissing Carole off." I told her. "But I don't think she'll complain too much. This school will be fundamental for Dahlia."

"What about after?" Lexi pressed. "How will you convince Dahlia to work here instead of continuing with her aunt?"

"Let me worry about that." I shrugged.

How will I convince her? I haven't thought that far ahead yet. I'm sure when the time comes, I'll devise the right words to persuade Dahlia. For now, I don't have to worry about it. It's a six-week program, giving me plenty of time.

The salon phone ringing temporarily cut off our conversation.

"Dagger Designs, how may I help you?" Lexi chirped. "May I inquire as to who is speaking?" She paused to listen, her eyes drifting to me. "I'm sorry, but she's stepped out. I can take a message and pass it along to her."

"Who was that?" I questioned after she hung up.

"Your future boyfriend." She held up her hands in defence. "That's the answer I received."

If someone's playing a prank, it's not funny. "Did he leave you any message?"

"Nope. He just called me a loyal guard, then hung up."

"Weird. I'll ask Ty if he can trace the call for me."

Lexi bit her lip. "Do you want me to ask him for you?"

I stared at her and watched the faintest shade of pink taint her cheeks. "Sure, go right ahead."

"I'll let you know what he finds."

With a nod, I returned to my office in the back of the salon. Turning from the hall into my office, I jumped back and quickly covered my mouth to muffle the escaped scream. Nico Frangione sat casually in my office chair. *What the hell is he doing here?* I glanced down the hall to the salon floor, verifying that no one saw or heard my reaction. I then slipped into the room and closed the door. Turning back to the intruder, I glared at Nico. He offered me a lazy, confident smile, and his eyes shone with lustful interest.

"Why are you here?" I demanded.

"I don't have your number." He responded with a casual shrug of his shoulders. "So, I came in person to ask you to lunch."

"No."

"No?" He cocked one dark brow.

"No." I repeated, crossing my arms. I didn't miss the quick trip south that his eyes took to my breasts before returning to meet my gaze. "I don't want to go to lunch with you."

"What about dinner? This Saturday."

"Not interested."

I'm not sure why I'm arguing. I am interested. Very interested. There's just something about him today that's put me on edge. It feels as though he's here for an ulterior reason than to ask me out.

"I'm interested." He told me.

He stood, coming around the desk. *Those suits have to be tailor-made.* My eyes roamed along his body, and on their path back up, I didn't miss the smirk playing on his lips. He knows precisely his effect on women, and I'm no different. My heart beat faster with each step closer he took. Nico stopped less than a foot away. I had to tilt my head up to keep eye contact with him. His gorgeously dark brown eyes reminded me of my parents' dark walnut dining room table. *I could stare into those eyes all day.*

"Why are you not interested?"

Having been lost in his eyes, it took me a moment to register his question. "Why are you interested?"

"I asked first."

"I'm all about first impressions, and yours didn't impress me." I lied.

My first impression of him is that he'd be excellent in bed. There's no way I'm telling him that.

"Do elaborate." He persisted.

"You seem like a playboy who only wants a woman to warm his bed and move on. I'm not interested in being a wham bam, thank you, ma'am."

Nico chuckled, his grin widening. "Wham bam, thank you, ma'am?"

I could feel the heat rising up my neck to my cheeks. "Are those words too difficult for you to understand?"

He shook his head and stepped even closer. "My turn. I'm interested because of your beauty, that mouth of yours, and because I don't want a woman for one night."

My breath caught. He was saying all the right things to make me — or any woman melt. *One dinner wouldn't kill me.* I opened my mouth to agree to a single dinner date but shut it immediately. I refuse to be swayed by pretty words so easily. Besides, I don't need him to warm my bed.

"At least allow me to offer you a preview of how our date could go." Nico offered softly.

Before I even questioned what he meant, Nico cupped the back of my neck and slanted his lips over mine. A burning awareness shot through me, every nerve ending awakened with his kiss. I have never felt such a thing before — not with my exes and not with Jaylen. Nico took full advantage of my slightly parted lips when I gasped by sliding his tongue into my mouth. I moaned. *This man can kiss.*

Uncurling my arms, I gripped his jacket lapels and leaned in. Nico wrapped his free arm around my waist, pressing our bodies closer. His kiss became needier. A wave of pure lust exploded between us in this one kiss where neither of us could get enough, yet we still held back. Nico fisted his hand in my hair and tugged my head back. A whimper slipped out.

"Dinner." He demanded, trailing kisses along my jaw. "Saturday."

"Nico."

I sighed when he sucked on my earlobe. He whispered in my ear, urging me to agree to the date. I couldn't respond. His kisses scrambled my brain cells. His lips trailed down my neck. He was finding that sensitive, sweet spot between neck and shoulder. I arched into him, my fingers curling more tightly into the fabric of his jacket.

"Say yes." He repeated on my skin. "One date to prove I'm not a playboy."

The word yes sat on the tip of my tongue. At that moment, my cell phone rang. The sound jolted me out of the daze I'd fallen into. I pushed Nico away. Going to the desk, I hesitated before picking up the device. *Didn't I leave it closer to this side?* My phone is currently sitting closer to my chair. Leaning over the desk, I picked up my ringing cell phone.

"Hello?"

"You okay, Rox?" Jaylen's questioning tone came from the other end. "You sound out of breath."

"Just ran to get the phone." I lied.

Nico came up behind me. He ran his hands up my arms. Brushing my hair to the side, he kissed my neck. I elbowed him, needing him to keep a distance so I could concentrate on the conversation. He ignored me. Instead, Nico brought his hands down my arms to cover my elbows and block other attacks. He did, however, stop kissing my neck.

"You didn't have to rush." Jaylen stated, redrawing my attention to him. "I would have just left a message."

"I'm here now." I glared at Nico from over my shoulder, and he just grinned.

"I was just calling to cancel our lunch plans. Ty and I are working on this massive case, and I can't seem to pull away today."

"That's okay, Jaylen. I'll see you tonight at least?"

"Definitely."

I hung up. Nico's chin rested on my shoulder. His large hands moved down to spread over my hips as he held me to him. It unnerved me how good it felt to be in his arms.

"Boyfriend?" He questioned, kissing my shoulder.

"Yes." I twisted in his arms to face him.

His brown eyes bore into mine. "Liar."

"Am not."

"If you had a serious boyfriend, you wouldn't have let me kiss you."

Nico kissed me again to prove his point. His fingers tightened on my hips. I could feel him trying to hold himself back. Some insane part of my mind begged him to let loose.

"If you had a boyfriend." He continued when he let my lips go. "You would have told me that right away instead of just telling me that you don't want to go for dinner with a possible playboy."

"Fine." I shoved at his chest, needing space from him. He moved half a step back. "He's not my boyfriend, officially. I'm still not going to go out with you."

"I think you will." His lips quirked into a smug grin.

I glared at him. "Why is that?"

Nico tilted my chin to brush his lips temptingly across mine again. My restraint was already at its limit. If he kissed me again, I may break down and agree to a dinner date. My fight against him is futile, and he knows it. Though, he may give up if I'm too much of a challenge. I heard the vibration of his phone. With a frown, Nico pulled back enough to check the message.

"I'll pick you up this Saturday at five."

Nico pecked my lips and left my office. With the door shut behind him, I slumped to the floor, my desk at my back, holding my chest. My poor heart. It beat so wildly that I thought it might pop out of my chest. *Stubborn, sexy man, I didn't agree to anything.*

Four

NICO

If it weren't for the text I'd received from Marco, I would have stayed with Roxanne, kissing her until she agreed to go on a date with me. As it stands right now, she hasn't agreed to anything. If neither of us had received phone calls or messages, I was certain clothes would have been shed. *Fuck.* That image didn't help tamper the hard-on I'm sporting.

Making my way back to my car, I caught sight of the unmarked cop car that had been following me this past month. I'd parked a few blocks away from Dagger Designs to throw them off my trail, but they found me. If they figured out where I'd gone, then word would get back to both Captain and Detective Baxter quickly, and my seduction plan would come to a sudden halt.

Returning to work, I took a moment to myself in the underground garage. Thankfully, only employees could enter. My tongue ran along my bottom lip. Roxanne's cotton candy taste still lingers there. My cock tightened in my pants even further. My plan today was to give her a light, teasing kiss, but the moment my lips touched hers, an electric zing raced through my body, and I needed more. I craved it. I might have come on strong, but Roxanne didn't seem to mind. *I need a cold shower.*

Stepping out of the car, I took the elevator straight up to the office floor of the building. The mirrored box showed me the wrinkles in my jacket from where Roxanne held me. I tried smoothing them out before the doors opened with no real luck. Only an iron would do it. Entering my office, I found Marco waiting. He lounged on the leather couch that's propped against the far wall for my late nights, playing on his phone. As a sales manager and friend, I wasn't sure which version I'd be dealing with,

Marco sat up, eyeing my appearance, and frowned. "You're arriving late this morning."

"I had an appointment."

"Did that appointment involve a pair of lips?" Marco grinned. "Your lips have a lip gloss sheen to them too."

Friend, I'm dealing with my friend. I ran my tongue over my lips. *I wonder if Roxanne would be submissive or wildly passionate in bed.* My body responded to the idea of her in my bed. Turning in an attempt to hide my body's reaction, I stiffly made it to my desk and sat down in the traditional tufted office chair. Its warm brown leather complements the heavy dark wood desk and shelving of the office. Marco got up from the couch only to plop his ass down in a chair across my desk. He still wore that stupid grin.

"I was trying to convince a woman to go on a date with me." I informed him flatly, though I couldn't hide the annoyance in my tone. "She stubbornly said no."

Marco laughed, slapping his knee. "Seriously? That has got to be a first. You've never had to convince a woman to go on a date with you before."

"Fuck off." I growled.

"She must really be something." Marco sobered — barely. "Especially since you've sworn off any form of relationship since Rachelle."

I winced at the name. "I'm not looking for a relationship."

"Really? Then why are you so pissed that this woman said no to a date?"

"I'm not pissed, just merely annoyed."

"Sure." He rolled his eyes. "It's not a bad thing to want a relationship. Just because Rachelle didn't work out doesn't mean the same thing will happen with this woman."

I stayed silent. *He doesn't know the half of it.* I haven't thought about Rachelle in years. Marco knows that I loved her. We dated in our final year of high school and for two years into college. I told him that Rachelle left the city to follow career opportunities. What Marco doesn't know is that my father is the reason she left — broken. I closed my eyes, my mood souring as Rachelle's tear-stained face surfaced in my mind. Re-opening my eyes, I frowned at my friend.

"Why are you here, Marco?"

"Two reasons." He pushed his square glasses up his nose, a goofy look on his face. "The first reason is that I want you to be the best man at my wedding."

"Your wedding?" I stared at him, processing the words. "When did that happen?"

"My woman asked me last night."

"Congratulations." I smiled, truly happy for my friend. "And I'd be honoured to be your best man."

"Excellent." He clapped his hands together, a serious expression now on his face. "Now, the other reason I'm here is that sales are up, and we could use some extra staff. I want to hire a couple more women who can upsell as well as Paige does. Also, I need some more staff for international sales. The demand for wanting particular and hard-to-find cars is rising."

"Do what you have to do to keep clients happy."

"Will do." He stood to leave. "Do let me know if you need help convincing this woman to go on a date with you. I've got a few ideas that'll be sure to convince her."

"Get to work." I growled.

Marco chuckled, heading out the door. With a sigh, I turned on the computer and then leaned back in my chair. *One kiss and this woman is already messing with my mind.* I need to know more about her to get the upper hand. It is difficult to seduce a woman I barely even know properly.

Logging into the computer, I pulled up Roxanne's social media pages. Something in here is bound to help me. There were plenty of posts about Dagger Designs. She posted life events and trips she's taken with her family. They never went far and would be able to return to Frostham within a day or two.

Roxanne made plenty of food posts. She even reposts one particular food blog called Just Yum. *So she likes food.* For all of her posts, Roxanne is pretty private. She didn't reveal anything too personal that I could use to seduce her. I stopped at a picture of her with a friend. The caption read that her friend was engaged as they showed off the diamond ring. The smile on Roxanne's face radiated her beauty. *Would she turn a smile like that on me?*

"Nico?"

I looked up to see Paige, my best saleswoman, at the door. Her voluptuous form and teasing flirtatiousness turned on any man, which helped her immensely to upsell the clients. Since she's been hired, Paige has been steadily working her way to my bed. I've taken her up on her no-strings sex offer but have never taken her to bed and never will. Looking at her now, after having Roxanne's body and lips pressed against mine, I don't find her as enticing.

"What can I do for you Paige?" I asked, maintaining a professional tone.

She closed the door to my office and sauntered closer, swaying her hips seductively. "You're looking a little stressed."

"A problem has risen." I trailed off, shifting in my seat.

"Is there anything I can do to help?" She batted her eyes

My cock's been hard since the kiss with Roxanne, and looking at pictures of her on her social media didn't help the situation. If I want to seduce Roxanne, I will need to focus on only her. No more fucking Paige in my office. Not even to relieve myself of the potential blue balls I probably have in my pants right now. Roxanne thinks I'm a playboy, and I will not indulge that misconception.

"I can resolve the issue on my own."

Paige licked her red lips, a smile curving them upward. "Let me help."

I closed the screen displaying Roxanne's smiling face. Paige came around the desk. She lifted her skirt to reveal her bare pussy, hopped on the desk and spread her legs. It's been a few months since I've fucked Paige in my office. As I stared, my hard-on lessoned.

"Clear your mind, Nico." Paige purred, her fingers dipping into her folds. "Let me take your stress away."

I closed my eyes, running a hand over my face. "You need to leave."

"What?"

I looked her in the eyes. "I'm not going to fuck you, Paige."

Paige slid off my desk slowly, stunned. I've never kicked her out before, never denied her of a good fuck. She pursed her lips and strode out. I opened the bottom drawer of my desk and stared at the box of condoms, only partially regretting my decision. *Roxanne will be worth it.* Until I can get Roxanne into bed, I predict I'll be taking many cold showers.

Five

ROXANNE

I STARED DOWN AT Jaylen's sleeping form. *How can he sleep so soundly?* I poked at his cheek while calling his name. The man had slept while I took a shower and got dressed. I even slammed drawers closed after opening them, hoping to rouse him. Jaylen groaned at my constant poking and cracked an eye open.

"You're dressed."

"How observant detective." I rolled my eyes.

"It's your day off."

"I have things to do."

Jaylen took hold of my wrist, pulling me back onto the bed as he rolled from his stomach to his back. "Without me?"

"You have to go to work. You have that massive case, remember?" I repositioned myself into a straddling position across his chest.

"How can a man work when he has a beautiful woman straddling him?"

I blushed. "You should be getting up."

"Already am." Jaylen gripped my hips, pushed me back and thrust upward.

"Jaylen." I groaned at the erection he pressed into me.

With an ego-filled grin, he rolled us over so I lay under him. His lips pressed to mine eagerly as he worked to remove my yoga pants. With a frustrated growl, he sat up to fully remove the tight fabric from my body. My snickers over his frustration turned into moans as his mouth went down on me. Blindly, I reached for the condoms stored on my bedside table. Jaylen chuckled when I threw some at him. He eagerly obeyed my demand and rolled one on.

I basked in the morning sex with Jaylen.

Skin sticky with sweat, I desperately needed another shower — one Jaylen joined me in. The water was beginning to get chilli by the time we got out. Nearly two hours had passed since my first shower for the day. I was re-dressed and heading out of my apartment with Jaylen. I walked down the three flights with Jaylen to the parking lot.

"Have a good day at work." I told him.

Typically, when Jaylen stays over, after the shower, he hops into his car and heads out. We have a friends-with-benefits relationship that has worked well for us this past year to scratch that sexual itch. So, I'm content when he doesn't show me any affection outside the bedroom. Something about him this morning seemed different. Today, Jaylen wrapped an arm around my waist, pulled me to him and kissed me. Outside. In the parking lot.

"You have a good day yourself." He said.

I stood there dumbfounded when he pulled away to head to his car. *What was that?* I watched the tail lights of his car disappear down the street. With a shake of my head, I unlocked my car and got in. I need to get started on my busy day. I can ponder Jaylen's behaviour while at the gym.

I parked at the three-story brick building on the edge of Frostham's industrial area. The business' name — Rocco's — is plastered above the door in simple black lettering. The outside may look non-descript, but the interior is modern and clean. This high-end fitness center has a high-end membership fee. One I don't mind paying. Rocco's has the newest equipment and a running track, just like so many other gyms in the city. What makes Rocco's unique is that it also has a few saunas, a swimming pool and my favourite — rock climbing walls.

I swiped my membership card at reception before heading to the locker room to toss my gym bag of clean clothes into the assigned locker. I might come for the rock climbing, but I know better than to start there. I started my exercise routine on the treadmill. A good three to five-kilometre jog is an excellent warmup.

I took the time to ponder Jaylen. It didn't matter which angle I looked at his actions from. I couldn't figure out why he kissed me. Outside. In public. I don't want to raise my hopes that he might want a real relationship with me.

Finished my run, I collected my water bottle and made my way to the door that led to the rock climbing. Dark eyes stared at me from the wall of mirrors I passed. *Nico.* A whirl of emotions had my steps faltering. I remembered the heat in his kiss the other day and how he made my body sing. The man smiled, put the weights he was using down and strolled over — pure male confidence in every step. My eyes roamed hungrily over his chest and arms, the t-shirt he wore accentuating his toned muscles.

"Hello again, Roxanne." He crooned.

I looked back up at him, standing my ground. Despite the great sex I had with Jaylen, both last night and this morning, my body reacted instantly to the sight of Nico. He looked good, glistening with sweat. I wanted him to be that way, not because of the weight but because he was pleasuring me in every way imaginable. *Get out of your head.* I berated myself. Trying to maintain a frosty demeanour, I crossed my arms. His charms will not sway me in any way.

"Nico." I responded as detached as possible.

"This is a wonderful surprise."

"I wouldn't call it wonderful."

Nico put a hand to his chest. The smile in his eyes contrasted with the playfully hurt expression on his face. "That wounds Roxanne."

I bit my cheek to stop myself from smiling. "What are you doing here?"

"Rocco's is the best fitness center in Frostham. Why wouldn't I be here?"

"I didn't mean to imply."Embarrassed, I cut myself off and turned away. "Sorry to have interrupted your workout. I'll let you continue."

"You're a pleasant interruption." He followed me. "Where are you off to now? The sauna? Or maybe the pool?"

"Do you really think I'd let you see me in a bathing suit?"

"A man can dream." He leaned in to whisper in my ear. "And I've dreamt of you."

My footing stumbled. I did not expect that answer, though I should have. Nico wrapped an arm around my waist to catch me.

"Careful."

"I'm okay." I pushed out of his hold and cleared my throat. "I'm going rock climbing."

"Preccato." Nico mumbled, then grinned. "I think I'll join you."

I yanked the door open, taking two steps at a time down a flight of stairs, opened another door, and entered the hall leading to the rock climbing. Nico followed — a silent shadow whose mere presence awakened every one of my nerve endings. I looked around at the various wall difficulties and decided to challenge myself. Slipping into a harness, one of Rocco's employees came around to inquire if I needed a spotter. Nico waved him off before I could utter a reply.

"What did you do that for?" I scolded.

"I'll be your spotter." He leaned in for a quick kiss. "Trust me."

"I don't trust you." My lips tingled, wanting another kiss. "I shouldn't trust you."

"Have a little faith, Roxanne. I can surprise you."

I stared at him, trying to decide my fate with this man. "If I fall, you're paying for my medical bills."

"I'd never let you fall."

Those words sounded more like a promise for something other than this situation. My heart skipped a beat. Turning to the wall, I focused on mapping my climb to the top. *He's just a sweet-talking player.* I told myself. *I deserve better.*

I waited for him to be ready to spot me before starting my climb. Nico kept the safety line perfectly. Not too loose that it'll be in the way and not too tight to hinder my climb. I was far too aware of Nico's eyes on me, and I lost focus on my accent. I found myself stuck on the underside of a curve. I gritted my teeth. *This wall will not beat me.*

"Do you need to come down?" Nico called up, a teasing note to his question.

"No." I accessed my situation more closely. "Give me about a foot of slack on the rope."

"Why?"

"Have a little faith, Nico." I threw his own words back at him. "I can surprise you."

The rope loosened with a chuckle from him. Adjusting my footing, I jumped for a rock hanging on the edge of the curve. Dangling there for a breath, I pulled myself up with both hands until one foot and each hand had their own rock to rest on. The bell at the top of this wall was still a few feet away to the left while I clung to the right side. The path to success is just out of reach. *I can do this, one more jump, and I'll be just about there.*

*DING*DING*

*DING*DING*

I beamed at my success. Nico tightened the safety line when the bell rang. Leaning back, I hopped down the wall. Once both feet were planted on the ground, I spun excitedly to Nico. My joy seized at the sight of him. His eyes had darkened with something dangerous and lust-fueled.

Taking a step back, I quickly looked away. I hurried out of the harness and ran to the locker rooms to escape. That dark look of his scared me. He scared me because that look pulled a visceral reaction in me. It made my breath catch and my heart speed up. I ran because I wanted to kiss him, wanted him to kiss me, wanted to peel his clothes off and do so much more than kiss. That look told me he wanted to do the same.

I took a shower for the third time today and changed into the clean clothes I'd brought. *Damn, I chipped a nail.* Sighing, I grabbed my now dirty gym bag and returned to my car. Before heading back home, I needed to go grocery shopping. I still have time before the appointment at the bridal shop.

Six

NICO

FINDING ROXANNE AT ROCCO'S was a coincidence. Not that she believed me. Her cold tone made me wonder if her family got to her. If that's the case, it'll make my seduction plan a little more challenging. I'd followed her to the rock-climbing wall, determined not to let this encounter go to waste.

Roxanne's ass, outlined by the harness, was a wondrous sight to behold. Then she went and nearly gave me a heart attack as she dangled from the edge of the rock-climbing wall, regardless of the fact that, as her spotter, I'd never let her fall. By the time her feet touched the ground, I wasn't sure what to say. I wanted to yell at her for scaring me and kiss her senseless, my relief of her being safely on the ground palpable. Then I wanted to fuck her, my body so turned on by her daredevil stunt. None of that mattered because she ran as fast as she could after one look at me.

Now, I sat parked in front of a coffee shop next to a bridal shop. According to the calendar I'd peeked at on her phone yesterday, she'd be here in twenty minutes for dress shopping. I planned to bump into Roxanne as I left the coffee shop, a chance meeting, but after our chance meeting at Rocco's, I wasn't so confident the plan would go over well. Just then, I saw Roxanne enter the coffee shop. *Fuck! There goes my plan.* I got out of the car, watching her through the window and just as she was coming out, I opened the door to the coffee shop.

"Thank you." She said, then frowned when she saw me. "Nico? Are you following me now?"

"Not at all." I smiled pleasantly.

"I find that hard to believe."

A woman with a stroller came up behind Roxanne. Taking hold of her elbow, I gently tugged her out of the way. When the woman entered the building, I let the door close. Roxanne didn't pull away from my touch. I'd count that as a small victory.

"You can let go of me now." She said the words but didn't attempt to move.

"I could." I tugged her closer and rested my hands on her hips. "Ma davvero non voglio."

Her brows knitted together. "What does that mean?"

"I really don't want to."

"Want to?" Roxanne's eyes widened as she realized the context. "But you have to let me go. I have somewhere to be."

You still have time. I thought while leaning in to wrap my lips around the straw of her drink. It was some caramel coffee concoction. Roxanne's breathing hitched. I swallowed the drink before taking possession of her lips. Her mouth opened for me instantly, and our tongues danced with each other.

I pulled back. "Not bad."

She blinked, her beautiful hazel eyes dilated. "Huh?"

"Your drink." I supplied, fighting back a knowing grin. "It's not bad."

"Oh." There was a hint of disappointment in that one word as her cheeks tinted pink.

"But I'd much rather drink from you." I whispered.

A visible shiver ran through her, and that blush intensified. "I told you I'm not a one-night stand kind of woman."

"Your exact words were wham bam, thank you, ma'am." I cupped her cheek, leaning in for another kiss.

"Same thing." Her breath came out in a soft sigh.

"I don't want you to be either of those." I brushed my lips on hers, desperately wanting another kiss, but she wouldn't stop talking. "You'll see. On our date Saturday, you'll get to know me better."

"I never agreed to a date." Roxanne stated soberly, pushing back.

"I'm taking you on one. Reservations have already been made." I lied.

"Unless those reservations are for Croquette, you're not taking me anywhere."

With that, Roxanne stepped out of my arms and turned to the bridal shop. *If you want Croquette, you'll get Croquette.* I returned to my car and drove to the French-style restaurant. Croquette is known for its three-month-long waiting list. Her little challenge will not stop me. Little does she know, my cousin owns the restaurant, so getting a table for this Saturday shouldn't be an issue.

I wandered around the back. The kitchen door was open, and my cousin stood there, keeping track of the ingredients entering his restaurant, checking things off on a clipboard.

"Hey Oliver."

"Nico!" He lowered the clipboard and pulled me into a hug. "What brings you by?"

"A favour."

"What kind of favour?"

"I need to make a reservation for this Saturday."

Oliver's green eyes lit up with amusement. "Hot date?"

"Yes." I answered with a grin. "She set me a challenge. Said she'd only go out with me if I have reservations for Croquette."

Oliver laughed. "Obviously, she has no idea that you have insider connections."

"Nope." My grin widened.

"Head on in and talk to Sonia. She handles all the reservations."

I slipped into the kitchen behind someone carrying a tray of tomatoes. The chef, sous chef, and a couple of other line cooks were verifying the quality of the ingredients and prepping for tonight's opening. Only being open for supper contributes to

Croquette's long reservation list. Quickly manoeuvring out of the kitchen and into the dining area, I searched for Oliver's wife. I found Sonia at the front podium reviewing a book.

Sonia turned. Her eyes widened with surprise before she smiled. "What are you doing here, Nico?"

"I'm hoping to get a reservation for this Saturday at six."

"For how many?" She turned back to the book, flipping through the pages.

"Two." I stepped up beside her.

Sonia's hand stopped, and she looked up at me again. "Two?"

"Yes, two."

"Nico Frangione." Her tone teasing. "Do you have a date?"

"Only if I can get a table this Saturday."

With a smile on her face, Sonia flipped two more pages of the book. "Six, you say. We can't do it. We're full. But I do have a table at five-thirty that's open."

"I'll take it."

Sonia wrote my name in the reservation book. "This woman must be special if you're bringing her here."

"She is." I agree, kissing Sonia on the cheek. "Grazie per questo."

"If the date goes well, Oliver and I want to meet her."

I chuckled. If things go well, I can get out from under my father. *Now, to find out where Roxanne lives.* I left the restaurant the same way I entered. I could have my hacker friend find the answer for me in a second. That's too easy. Roxanne needs to know I tried. My police tail followed me from Croquette to Dagger Designs. This time, I didn't bother trying to lose them. It was becoming too much of an effort. Roxanne's blonde receptionist looked up when I walked into the salon. Her blue eyes widened slightly, but otherwise, she kept a pleasant, professional expression.

"Welcome back to Dagger Designs. How may I help you?"

"I'm Roxanne's future boyfriend." I extended my hand. "Nico Frangione."

The woman laughed while accepting my hand. "So, you're my mysterious caller."

"I am. And you are?"

"Lexi Dawson. What brings you in today Nico?"

"Any chance I can convince you to provide me with Roxanne's address?" I threw her a charming smile.

"Nope."

I leaned forward on the counter. "What about a bribe?"

Lexi crossed her arms. "I'm her loyal guard, remember?"

I laughed. "Indeed, you are. I have a date with Roxanne this Saturday, and I told her I'd pick her up. The thing is, I don't know where she lives, and asking her feels like it'll spoil the romantic gesture."

"You got Rox to agree to a date?" Lexi leaned forward. A mixture of doubt and curiousness was evident in her tone. "Where are you taking her?"

"Croquette."

"Try again. Croquette has a three-month waiting list."

I stepped away from the counter when a new client walked in. Lexi confirmed the appointment and directed her to the waiting area, and then another client stepped up to pay. She processed the transaction and talked to an employee about her next appointment. *Where did Roxanne find her?* If she weren't Roxanne's, I'd probably try to poach her for my own business. The woman was professional and efficient and could jump from one conversation to another without missing a beat.

I returned to my leaning spot, picking up our conversation. "Honestly, I have reservations for this Saturday at five thirty."

Lexi shook her head. "Pretend I do believe you. What makes you think I'll tell you Rox's address?"

"Because you want your boss to go on a date with someone as good-looking as me and go eat at one of the most exclusive restaurants in Frostham." I flashed her a cocky smile.

Lexi only laughed. "Nice try, Nico."

I didn't think that would work. "Why won't you provide me with Roxanne's address?"

"It's not mine to provide."

"Would you give it to me if I'd lost it and was too embarrassed to ask for it again?"

"Nope." She made a popping sound with the p.

I let out a playfully frustrated sigh. "Fine. It was nice meeting you, loyal guard Lexi."

"And you, future boyfriend Nico."

That didn't go my way. I can generally charm any woman. Lexi now makes the second woman I haven't been able to persuade this week. I returned to my penthouse. A text was sent to my hacker friend about getting Roxanne's address. It didn't surprise me when the answer came within minutes. I made myself something to eat, took a shower to freshen up, then went back out.

The cops followed me to a public parking garage three blocks from where I wanted to be. The cops drove by where I parked and kept going up. It gave me a short window to get to my destination. They don't know that my destination is Bella Luna.

About a month before I stepped away from Obsidian, Bella Luna opened its doors. From day one, the two dance clubs have been rivals, both competing to be known as the best in Frostham. On paper, the club is owned by Darryl Keen. In reality, I own it. I had caught Darryl snooping around Obsidian. When confronted, he admitted he wanted to own a club and was looking around Obsidian for ways to make his club just as successful. Obsidian was never mine. It was more of a family business. I struck up a deal with Darryl; I'll help him open up his club as long as I could be a silent owner. I didn't want my family — especially my father — to learn about my involvement in Bella Luna. They'd only get their dirty hands involved.

From time to time, I stop by to see how the club is doing. The first floor of Bella Luna hosts the dance floor and a bar with a few small tables for people to stand at. The second floor has another bar and private booths with a view of the dance floor below. The third floor has the security office, employee lounge, and Darryl's office. I stopped by the first-floor bar for a drink and surveyed the crowd.

Cristo. I stood a little straighter, my eyes laser-focused on Roxanne Baxter. She stood at a small table with three other women. Her back was to me, but I'd recognize her anywhere. Roxanne's honey-blonde hair was tied up in a high ponytail, exposing her perfectly kissable neck. My eyes trailed down the length of her body, appreciating the green dress that hugged her every curve, and ended only a few inches lower than her ass. Matched with knee-high boots, the dress appeared even shorter than it actually was. *I wonder if she's wearing anything under that dress.*

A primal urge to go to her tugged at me. I had to use every ounce of control not to move from my spot. Two of her friends wandered off to the dance floor. Roxanne chatted with the other woman for a bit before she chugged her drink and then tugged the friend to the dance floor. I wanted to be out there with her, have her body pressed tightly against mine as we gyrated to the beat pulsing throughout the club. *She's with friends.* I scolded myself, shaking my head and forcing myself to the third floor.

"Nico." Darryl greeted me warmly. "It's been a while."

"Darryl." I gestured to the couch. "How have things been here?"

"Excellent. Every night, the club is packed." He joined me. "There are minor drunken scuffles, but nothing security can't handle."

"That's good."

"What brings you to the club tonight?"

The couches sat opposite each other. The floor between them is a thick piece of glass, allowing us to see directly above the dance floor. With the strobing lights, no one would be able to see the office, not even from the second floor. I watched the crowd below, automatically finding Roxanne. She looked to be having fun dancing with her friends.

"I just needed a change of pace." I finally answered Darryl.

He grinned. "Looking for someone to take home?"

Only Roxanne will do. I shook my head. "While I'm here, I want to review the reports."

"Of course."

Darryl put his drink down on the side table and got up from the couch. I watched Roxanne on the dance floor until Darryl handed me last month's reports. I reviewed everything. Income, expenses, which nights were the busiest, what alcohol was used the most, and so on. Nothing appeared out of the ordinary, which means the family hasn't gotten wind of Bella Luna being mine yet. *I hope it stays that way.* I'm always afraid they're going to get their hands on this place.

"Looks good." I handed the reports back.

"Running this club has been a dream." Darryl returned the reports to the filing cabinet and then came back to sit on the couch. "I know it's been a couple of years, but I really can't thank you enough."

"Keeping this place clean and its doors open is thanks enough."

Darryl's hazel eyes sparkled. "If it weren't for this club, I would have never met my girlfriend."

"Oh?" I raised a brow while taking a sip of my scotch.

"I met her last month. I saw her from up here, went down to dance with her, and that's how we met."

"You don't seem like the kind of man who'd melt at some woman's swaying hips."

"It wasn't her swaying hips that got me to the dance floor." Darryl chuckled. "She's a librarian — wicked smart, funny, and kind. The night we met was the first time she'd been out with friends in months. A dance club isn't really her scene, but they dragged her along anyway."

"I bet she's glad they brought her along."

"I'm glad they did."

"I'm happy for you."

We fell into a comfortable silence. My eyes drifted back to the dance floor, finding Roxanne with some guy. *Fuck no.* I chugged my scotch and rushed down to the first floor. The possessiveness rearing inside for Roxanne is an odd feeling. I chopped it up to my plan to seduce her. If some other guy seduces her first, then I won't be able to use her. I shoved people out of my way in my need to get to Roxanne. The guy she was dancing with had his hands on her hips and held her close to him. Too close. Coming up behind Roxanne, I wrapped an arm around her waist and tugged her flush against my body. She didn't resist.

"Hey, buddy, we were dancing." The guy complained.

"Not anymore." I growled.

"You had your dance." Roxanne stated as she leaned into me.

The guy looked dumbfounded, then pissed when he stormed off the dance floor. I couldn't help the smug smile curving my lips. Roxanne reached up, her fingertips brushing along my neck, and her body swayed to the music.

"Dance with me." She purred.

Then she bent forward, wiggling her ass against my groin. She had a mischievous smile on her lips when she looked over her shoulder at me. *One dance.* With a groan, I hauled her back up and moved with her. The club was warm with the number of bodies in the room, but with Roxanne in my arms, I was on fire.

I had to get off the dance floor. As one song melted into another, I tugged Roxanne to the second floor so we could have a little bit of privacy. A waitress took drink orders and then returned shortly with the alcohol — a martini for Roxanne and a second scotch for myself.

"Why are you here, Nico?" Her gaze was suspicious.

"Does it matter?"

"I'm curious."

I pulled her legs onto my lap, eliciting a little squeak from her. I rested a hand on her legs to prevent her from moving away while I picked up my drink with my free hand. Roxanne's chest heaved beneath the fabric of her dress. I watched her out of the corner of my eye as she watched me, waiting for an answer.

"I'm curious, too." I told her.

"About what?" She sipped her martini.

I slid my hand up her leg, trailing my fingers along the bottom of her dress. Roxanne put her drink back on the table. She closed her eyes, put her hands on the seat behind her and leaned back slightly.

"I'm curious. Are you wearing any panties?" I asked her in a low, seductive tone. "Voglio vedere."

She bit her bottom lip. I could see the debate in her eyes when she opened them. Let me find out, or keep me in suspense. Roxanne opened her legs slightly. I slipped my hand between her legs. Before I could trail my hand any higher than the hemline, she closed her legs, trapping my hand. Roxanne sat up and leaned in close.

"You'll never know." She whispered.

I stole a quick kiss. "Not tonight, at least."

"So cocky."

"You haven't seen anything yet."

I pulled my hand out from between her thighs. Taking hold of her hips, I lifted her onto my lap. *This is where she belongs.* With an arm around her waist, I reached for my scotch. Roxanne took the drink from me. Eyes locked with mine, she sipped the amber liquid, swallowed, and then kissed me.

Taking the glass from her, I put it on the table before cupping the back of her neck. She parted her lips, allowing my tongue to dive in. Roxanne tasted spicy, like the scotch, and something that was purely her. It was intoxicating. She knitted her fingers in my hair, nails scrapping against my skull, kissing me back with as much eagerness. My cock strained against the zipper of my pants painfully. I want so much more from this woman.

Roxanne shifted. I groaned while tightening my hold on her. Ignoring my silent demand for her not to move, she repositioned herself to straddle my lap. The action had her short dress rising. My hands trailed down to her ass, pushing the fabric down to keep her covered and squeezed. She fit perfectly in my hand.

"Scopami." I mumbled. "Per favore, Bella."

She is far too tempting. I pressed her against me, wanting to be inside her. Roxanne moaned. Her off-shoulder dress provided me clear access to her neck. I trailed my lips down the column of her neck and followed the edge of her dress. Roxanne arched, raising those perfect mounds higher.

Her hands tightened in my hair as I trailed kisses across her chest. "Nico."

"I know." I murmured against her skin.

I kissed a trail up the other side of her neck and back to those perfectly plump lips of hers. *Now is not the time for more.* Roxanne rocked into me. I let out a frustrated groan.

"Roxanne." I shook my head. "Bella, stop moving, or else I'll do something you'll regret in the morning."

"Maybe." She nipped my ear.

Roxanne trailed her hands from my hair, over my shoulders, then down my chest. Her fingers worked on the buttons of my shirt, opening it wider for her lips to trail to my collarbone. *This woman is going to be the death of me.* It took willpower to clasp her hands and lift her head. Heavy-lidded hazel eyes looked at me.

"Bella, if you continue, I won't be able to hold back. You deserve more than a fuck in a private booth in a club." I set her on the seat next to me, making sure that the skimpy dress covered her. "I want to take you out on a date first. Prove to you I'm not a playboy." I took her hand and kissed the palm, taking satisfaction when her breathing hitched. "Cristo donna. When I do fuck you, it'll be in my bed where I can take my time kissing every inch of you. I'll get you so worked up that when I do slide my cock into your pussy you'll shatter for me instantly."

Roxanne closed her eyes and shivered. That reaction from her boosted my ego. *Does my woman enjoy a little dirty talk?* She opened her eyes, anticipation lingering in her gaze.

"When I take you for the first time." I continued. "It'll be world record-breaking. Every time after that, the bar will continue to rise."

"Playboy knows how to talk the talk." She teased.

"When you go home tonight, Bella, you're going to play with yourself, and when you do, you'll think of me." I let her go reluctantly. "Now, go back to your friends. I'll see you Saturday for our date."

Roxanne's cheeks reddened when I told her to play with herself, but when I mentioned her friends, her expression cleared. Horror filled her eyes as if she couldn't believe she'd wandered away from them. I watched Roxanne scurry out of the booth. I needed to get home myself and take an ice-cold shower.

Seven

ROXANNE

JAYLEN WAS ALREADY GONE by the time I woke up. He was more than willing to let me into his bed after the club. Sadly, I couldn't get Nico out of my mind. Now that the sun had risen and my head was clearer, I didn't want to get out of bed. My interaction with Nico at the club last night was embarrassing. I couldn't believe how forward I was. *Stupid alcohol. Stupid, sexy man.* I can't get my head on straight when it comes to Nico when sober, and apparently, my body takes control of my actions when alcohol is in the mix.

I punched the off button on the alarm with a groan. It's Saturday. Unfortunately, the clock had begun its countdown for when Nico said he'd pick me up. Lexi had rearranged my day's schedule so I'd have the afternoon off. It would give me plenty of time to get ready for my date. A date that I'm not mentally prepared for.

After my last client, I came straight home. I locked my apartment behind me, kicked off my shoes and trudged toward my bedroom. I froze at the edge of the kitchen. My brother and his partner sat at the kitchenette. Both men looked up at me, neither one of them smiling. *This can't be good.*

"Why are you here?" I demanded, not wanting to deal with either of them today.

"Nico Frangione." Jaylen said bitterly.

Do they know about my date? I frowned. "I don't understand."

"You've been seen with him on multiple occasions." Tyler explained. "And he's been to Dagger Designs. I talked to Lexi. She said you have a date with him tonight."

"So?"

I walked to my bedroom to put my purse away. They followed. I turned to my closet to find an outfit for tonight. I'm already on edge about this date, and I do not need them to add to those nerves.

"Why are you here?" I repeated, needing to know more specifics.

"Nico Frangione is a suspect in a multi-department investigation."

I pulled out a dress and turned to my brother. "Which departments?"

"Narcotics, Missing Persons, and Homicide." Tyler answered.

Bile rose in my throat, and I fought to swallow it back down. "I didn't know."

"Why are you going on a date with him in the first place?" Jaylen demanded.

"Because he asked me out." I glared at him.

I shouldn't be bitter about that. Jaylen and I have an understanding. Our friends-with-benefits relationship is private. Dates are for people in relationships or wanting to connect with someone. We're not in that kind of relationship. Going out for supper isn't in our verbal agreement.

"You should have said no."

"Gee, why didn't I think of that?" I bit out sarcastically with a roll of my eyes. Sitting on the bed, I looked up at my brother. "What should I do, Ty?"

He ran a hand through his dirty blond hair with a sigh. "Go on the date."

"What?" I squeaked, turning wide eyes to Jaylen. "He's kidding, right?"

Jaylen studied his partner before answering. "No, he's not. Are you out of your mind, Ty? We want to keep Rox away from Nico, not propel her into his arms."

"I don't want my little sister anywhere near this criminal." Tyler ground out. "But we also can't let this opportunity slip by."

"Opportunity?" Jaylen repeated, eyes wide as he realized what my brother was thinking. "Fuck no. I am strongly against it."

"So am I, but we can't let feelings cloud our judgment."

"Time out." I stood, my hands in the universal 'time out' symbol. "You two are talking in code. The only part I understand is that it involves me."

"Roxanne." Tyler held my shoulders, staring at me with his serious cop face. "I want you to be our inside woman."

"Inside woman?"

He nodded. "Go on this date wearing a wire. Woo him, become his girlfriend, feed us inside information."

I stared at my brother like he's gone insane. "No."

"Please, Rox."

"Absolutely not. You just told me Nico's dealing drugs, kidnapping people, and is a murderer."

Tyler winced. "None of that is confirmed. Well, it is, and it isn't."

"What does that mean?"

"Narcotics has infiltrated the drug ring. In the past four years, they can only confirm that Mr. Frangione is in charge and that the money drop-offs happen at Obsidian." Jaylen explained. "The missing women have all been seen last at the same club over the last two years, and the bartender at the club was murdered just over a month ago."

"What makes you think it's Nico, then?" I asked.

"He owns the club."

My throat tightened. Now I understand. That doesn't mean Nico is involved with any of that stuff. My mind spun with what they were saying. The man I've been dealing with this week is nothing like the man they are describing. Though, I could be blinded by lust.

"We don't know which department is involved, but they have someone deep undercover with the family." Tyler continued. "And we've had Nico tailed since the murder. In all those years, no one has been able to get proof of Nico's hands in these crimes, nor has anyone gotten as close as you have."

Tyler pleaded with his eyes. *Holy shit.* It was a lot to take in. My date with Nico was fast approaching. I don't have time to process any of it. Jaylen and Tyler watched me. They were waiting for my answer. I know they broke protocol by telling me about these active cases. The risk will only pay off if I agree to help.

I sank back down onto my bed. "Does Dad know about this?"

"I didn't tell him about you being caught in surveillance shots." Tyler reassured me.

"The captain wants the Frangione's taken down." Jaylen added. "By any means necessary. He also believes Nico is the weak link in the family."

"Okay." I took a deep breath, steeling myself for what was to come. "I will wear a wire during this date. After, I will decide if I'll be your inside woman. I need to think it over, make sure nothing will affect my salon or my employees."

"Deal." Ty nodded. "But I'll need an answer in twenty-four hours."

I nodded. Tyler left my bedroom only to return with a black case. He placed it on the bed, opening it to reveal tech stuff. He held up a small box with a long wire attached.

"I know it's old school." Tyler began. "But this is the only way to ensure that there's no tampering with any evidence. The microphone will be tapped to your chest, and the recording box will be at your back."

I stared at the box. It was about the size of a deck of cards. "Am I supposed to put it on myself?"

"One of us should put it on to make sure it's properly secure." Jaylen answered, then turned to Tyler. "Do you want to do it?"

"I'm not looking at my sister in her underwear." Tyler shoved the device into Jaylen's chest. "You better keep your eyes on the job, not on her."

With that warning, my brother left my bedroom. Jaylen and I smiled at each other. The warning was pointless, but Tyler didn't know that. I stripped out of my jeans and t-shirt, watching with amusement as his eyes lit up with lust. Because I could, I teased him further by stripping out of the cotton bra and panties and changing to a lace set. The bra had to switch to strapless for the dress anyway. Jaylen stepped closer, his eyes locked on mine. His fingers slid under my bra, between my breasts. He didn't linger as he placed the microphone. The wire wrapped around my torso twice before he stepped around me to tape the recording box to my lower back. For added insurance, he taped the wire in a couple of spots to keep it from moving.

Coming back around, Jaylen cupped my face and kissed me. Slowly, deeply. I tilted my head back and leaned into him. My fingers hooked into the belt loops of his jeans. Jaylen smiled and pulled back.

"Get dressed."

With that order, he left me. *What the hell?* Now, I'm even more perplexed. This out-of-character demeanour with Jaylen needs to be explained. First, it was the kiss out in public the other day before he went to work. Now, with a sweet kiss while my brother is not far away. If it weren't for Tyler's voice on the other side of the door, I would have stormed out to demand an explanation.

I shook my head, forcing myself to turn from the door and finish getting dressed for my date. With Nico. With a suspected murderer and drug dealer. My stomach tightened. Nico doesn't seem like the murdering, drug dealer type. However, I did peg him as a playboy when I first met him. It might have been a lie then, but it seems believable now. Maybe that's how he lures people in and gets their defences down. Maybe I'm his next target.

I stared at myself in my bathroom mirror. *I can do this.* Ty and Jaylen will listen in and come for me if I'm in danger. I'm also not defenceless. Tyler taught me self-defence back in high school and goes over a practice run yearly with me. My overprotective brother knows I won't go down without a fight.

I can do this. I reminded myself again before filling a clutch with ID, phone, and keys. I pulled out a pair of black pumps with a cute bow on the back from my closet and then left the safety of my bedroom. Jaylen and Tyler sat at the kitchenette. Both men frowned, but Jaylen's green eyes darkened with appreciation.

"What do I need to know about this recording device?" I questioned, my hand tapping the box at my back.

"Jaylen would have turned it on when he put it on you." Tyler explained. "We'll be listening in and following at a distance."

"If it sounds like you're in danger, we'll come rushing in." Jaylen informed.

"Okay." I nodded.

"Try to get Nico to talk — anything we can use. But be careful. We don't want him to get suspicious." Ty continued.

"Okay."

There was a knock on my apartment door. We all froze. I looked at the stove clock: four forty-five. It's too early for Nico, though it could still be him. I went to answer the door.

"Nico." My heart fluttered at the sight of him.

The man smiled down at me. "Evening, Bella, you look stunning."

"You're earlier than expected."

"I was excited to see you again."

I narrowed my eyes at him. "Do I want to know how you got my address?"

"Probably not."

I knew he'd get my address somehow, even if Lexi wouldn't give it to him. Using my clutch, I pushed him further into the hall so I could lock my apartment. When Jaylen and Tyler leave, they will lock it with their key. Nico offered me his elbow. Hesitantly, I slipped my arm through, and he walked me out of my apartment building. A black sedan sat waiting in the lot, and a chauffeur stood by the back door, opening it as we approached. I slid to the far seat and buckled in.

"Why me?" I questioned after we'd been silent for a few blocks.

"Excuse me?" Nico raised a brow, shifting in his seat to face me better.

"Why me?" I repeated. "You could have any number of women sitting here, going on a date with you, but you've stubbornly decided on me. I want to know why."

"I believe I told you the reason in your office earlier this week."

"Not exactly. You said you're interested because of my beauty and my mouth and that you don't want a one-night stand. Any of those reasons can describe plenty of women in Frostham. So, why me?"

Nico stared at me a moment. "Very well, Bella."

"Don't call me that." I told him sternly, needing to put up barriers against his charm. "If I'm not mistaken, that's a term of endearment, and we are not in any form of relationship where that is acceptable."

"Come si desidera Roxanne."

I frowned at him. "What does that mean?"

"As you wish."

A secretive little grin lifted his lips, and my insides fluttered. I've never considered another language to be sexy before. When Nico speaks Italian, I have an urge to act like Gomez when Morticia speaks French — kiss him all over. With his looks and voice, the woman in me has difficulty resisting our proximity. *He's a potential murderer.* I reminded myself in an attempt to cool my libido.

"Thank you." I managed to say. "Now, about why you asked me out."

"My interest was first peaked when you stood up to my sister." He indulged. "So many either give in to her demands or try to butter her up. Her social media influence is extensive, and people fear what she'll do to them. Then we locked eyes, and you took my breath away."

I rolled my eyes.

Nico chuckled. "I know it's cliché, but that's what happened. What you did next, or didn't do actually, intrigued me."

"Which was?"

"You didn't swoon."

Despite myself, I laughed. "Must have been a first."

"It was actually." He answered seriously. "I won't lie. There have been many women in the past. Every weekend, I could have someone new. None of them were real, and they only wanted something from me. I felt like I was missing something. For the past two years, I've turned down the women who batted their eyes and offered themselves up for a good time — mostly." Nico smiled softly. "Then I met you. The first woman to catch my interest in a very long time and the first to say no."

There was honesty and pain in his tone. His shoulders had slumped as he told his story, and his eyes revealed the loneliness he'd felt all those years. My heart went out to him. I know how he feels. Even with Jaylen in my bed, I still feel lonely. I want someone to love and cherish me like my parents love each other. I want forever with someone.

The car stopped. I heard the chauffeur get out, and within seconds, he opened the car door. Nico got out first, then offered me a hand. I hesitated a moment before slipping my hand into his. I stared up at the awning for Croquette.

"You were serious." I looked at Nico. "Lexi said you got reservations for Croquette."

A cocky grin lit Nico's face. "As requested."

"How? There's a three-month wait list."

"Trust me."

Nico placed a hand on my back, not too low, guiding me inside. The restaurant was dimly lit, with soft instrumental music playing through speakers to give a romantic atmosphere. The hostess led us to the second floor. Nico pulled out my chair, helping me sit before he moved over to his chair. The hostess handed us a single-page menu and informed us our waiter would be with us momentarily before returning to her post.

I stared at the menu. *How am I supposed to choose when it all sounds delicious?* I'm tempted to order everything since I doubt I'll come here again. But that would be rude of me. The waiter came around, and Nico immediately ordered a bottle of red wine and handed over his credit card. I frowned at him.

"This way, we don't have to wait for the bill at the end." Nico explained.

The waiter returned with the requested bottle, pouring a little into a glass. "Here you are, sir."

Nico swirled the wine and then took the sip that was provided. "That'll do quite nicely."

"Very well." The waiter began filling both wine glasses on the table. "Have you decided on a meal, or do you wish to have another minute?"

"Roxanne?"

I scanned the menu one more time. "I think I've decided."

"What will the lady have tonight?" The waiter inquired, setting the bottle down.

"I'll have the flamiche."

"Excellent choice." He took the menu. "And for you, sir?"

"We'll start with the baked brie, then I'll have the beef bourguignon."

"Do either of you wish to order dessert now?"

"Chocolate soufflé, please." I answered instantly.

Nico chuckled. "Tarte Tatin for myself."

"Excellent selections." The waiter smiled and left.

"I've heard great things about this restaurant." I commented while reaching for my wine.

"The chef uses fresh and local as much as possible. Because of that, the menu changes seasonally." Nico explained.

"You got that off their website." I scolded lightly.

Nico grinned, unashamed. "Here, I thought I could impress you with my knowledge. Throw a little mystery in this relationship."

"We're not in a relationship." I reminded him.

"Not yet." He proclaimed.

"We know nothing about each other aside from our names."

"All that will change tonight. Tell me, Roxanne, why did you name your salon Dagger Designs? It's a unique name for a nail place."

"My brother." I smiled wistfully. "He used to always call my nails daggers. He still does, actually."

"You have a brother? Is he older or younger? Do you have any other siblings?"

"Older by two years."

The waiter came to place the appetizer Nico ordered down in the center of the table. I leaned in, inhaling the delicious scent. With a simple 'enjoy' from the waiter, he left us alone again. I picked up the knife that came with the dish and spread the soft cheese onto thinly sliced and toasted baguette pieces. The rosemary baked with the Bree added to its natural nuttiness without overpowering the cheese, and the contrasting textures of cheese to baguette are perfect. I couldn't resist closing my eyes and moaning.

"That good?" Nico chuckled.

I opened my eyes, embarrassed. "I'm sorry."

"Don't be." He served himself some cheese. "Even if this date ends on a bitter note, which I hope it doesn't, at least you enjoyed the food at the restaurant you chose."

"Tell me about your family." I changed the subject. "Is Candi your only sibling?"

"Candi is younger by three years. I do have a brother, older by three years as well." Nico's tone turned bitter. "We aren't especially close. He's always been our father's favourite and is following in his footsteps."

"I'm sorry." I reached across the table to place a hand over his. "That must have been hard."

Nico shifted his hand so our fingers laced together. "When I was young, yes, it was hard. I wanted my father's approval. Then Candi came into the picture. Our mom died when she was eight, and I took it upon myself to protect her. The older I got, the less I wanted my father's approval and the more he wanted to bring me into the family business."

"Oh? What does your family do?"

"Nothing important. I want nothing to do with them. That's why I opened my luxury car dealership. I've made it grow on my own with no influence from my father or brother."

I squeezed his hand lightly before pulling away to serve myself more brie. The emotion he conveyed felt sincere. He really doesn't like his brother or father. *There's no way the man before me is a murderer.* Maybe Tyler and Jaylen have the wrong Frangione. I've been trying to fight my attraction toward Nico since he picked me up, and that story sealed my fate.

Eight

NICO

"TELL ME A LITTLE about your family." I prodded, needing to steer her focus off my family.

"Not much to say. I have a tiny family — extended family included. My mom is a stay-at-home woman. My dad is a prominent member of society. Meanwhile, my overprotective brother is following in our dad's footsteps. My parents supported me when I decided to open my own business." She shrugged. "We're a tight-knit, loving family."

"What does your father and brother do?"

Roxanne shook her head, a smile playing on her lips. "You didn't tell me what your family does, so I'm not telling you what mine does."

I chuckled. "Fair is fair."

The waiter returned to remove the empty appetizer and informed us our main course would be served shortly. He even refilled our wine glasses. I'm assuming what I felt on Roxanne's back is a listening device. If I'm right, I have to be careful as to what I say.

"Let's play a game." She suggested. "Twenty questions. We have to answer every question before the other asks the next question. This way, we can get to know each other."

"Okay, ladies, first." I took a sip of wine, tensing, uncertain as to what her first question would be.

Roxanne pondered her question, then smiled. "What is your favourite colour?"

I appreciated Roxanne's question, my shoulders relaxing. The questions we asked during the game were light and playful. She didn't try to pry any further into my family too much, either. At first, Roxanne seemed cold and distant, trying to keep whatever she was told by either her father or brother in the forefront of her mind. When I told her the littlest bit about my family, something seemed to change. It was like she decided to have fun on this date and pretend she didn't learn anything about me from someone else.

"Any hobbies?" Roxanne asked the following question.

"Nothing in particular. I find exercise a great way to relieve stress. You?"

"Rock climbing and puzzles."

"Somehow, I'm not surprised by that answer." I chuckled. "When your feet hit the ground the other day, you were beaming with pride at ringing that bell."

She smiled widely. "I love the challenge it brings and, of course, succeeding."

The waiter came by with our food. Roxanne leaned in, smelling the aromas before picking up her fork. The first bite went into that luscious mouth of hers, and her eyes closed. She pulled the utensil out with a moan. A moan that went straight to my cock. *This woman makes food sexy.* I've had a hard-on since that first moan with the appetizer. With her, it's rather difficult not to have one.

"Here." I offered her my fork after she's swallowed. "Try this."

Locking eyes with me, she leaned forward, put a hand around mine and guided the bite of food to her mouth. She closed her lips around the tongs and sucked the food off with a moan. A moan so addictive I desperately want to hear it again and again, but when my mouth is on her body.

"Delicious." She licked her lips.

I swallowed hard. "You're making it very difficult to stay gentlemanly."

"Am I?"

Roxanne batted her eyes innocently, a teasing smile on her lips. A surprising growl rumbled out with my affirmative answer. Roxanne shifted in her seat, a blush rising to her cheeks. The things my mind conjured to do to this woman did not help my current dilemma. Unable to hold my gaze, she lowered her eyes to her plate and continued to eat. Needing to lessen the pressure in my pants, I also returned to my food and picked up our game of twenty questions.

By the time the main course finished, Roxanne was leaning in and smiling, entirely at ease with me. She wore that same radiant smile she had in her social media pictures. I laced my fingers with hers. Touching her eases something within me, something I can't explain. When dessert came, Roxanne ate her chocolate soufflé with one hand, keeping her other hand linked with mine. At the first bite, she shimmied in her seat.

"Good?" I questioned with a chuckle.

"I love a good decadent chocolate dessert."

"Good to know."

She narrowed her eyes at me. "Why is that good to know?"

"I have our next three dates planned."

"Three dates?" Her shock caused her voice to go up an octave. "I don't recall agreeing to a second date with you."

"By the time I return you to your front door tonight, you'll agree to another date with me."

"That's some ego you have, Nico."

"Not ego." I corrected. "Confidence. Most women find it sexy."

Roxanne laughed. "I'm not most women."

"No, you are not." I lowered my voice seductively.

Again, she blushed. *I wonder how far down that blush goes.* We finished our dessert and then left the restaurant. Roxanne allowed me to wrap an arm around her waist. *Perfect fit.* I chose to ignore the recording device. My driver was already out front waiting for us. This time, Roxanne sat next to me in the car, leaning into me instead of sitting as far from me as possible. I slung my arm around her, keeping her close.

"I believe we have three more questions in our little game."

"And it's your turn." Roxanne acknowledged.

"Hmm." I mused, running my fingers lightly up and down her arm. "If you could go anywhere in the world for a two-week vacation, where would it be?"

"Hard to pick just one place. There are so many places to visit." She bit her lower lip. "I've dreamt of touring Europe, but that's a three to four-week vacation I can't afford."

"Where in Europe are you most wanting to go?" I prodded.

"Either France or Italy. I'm not sure which one I'd like to see more."

"May I suggest Italy? You'd love the food and the picturesque towns that are not on any tourist map."

"Sounds delightful. What about you? Where would you go?"

I cupped her face, angling up so I could stare down into those beautiful hazel eyes of hers. "Anywhere, as long as I'm with you."

Roxanne's breath caught, and her lips parted slightly. I leaned in to kiss her. A slow, passionate kiss. She reached up, her fingernails grazing the back of my neck and holding me in place. It took all my willpower not to pull her onto my lap and deepen the kiss. The car came to a stop, and I forced myself to pull back.

"Come on, our date isn't over yet."

Roxanne blinked back the lust in her gaze. "Where are we?"

The car door opened, and I helped her out. "Movie theatre."

She laughed. "Dinner and a movie? How very normal."

"That sounded like an insult."

"Just a statement."

"Well, this date is so we can get to know each other better. The next date will be much more tailored."

"You're getting ahead of yourself, Nico." She leaned into me. "What movie are we seeing? Or do I get to choose?"

"Tickets are already purchased."

"So, what movie are we seeing?"

"You'll see shortly." I replied while guiding her into the movie theatre. "I think you'll approve."

I pulled out my phone so the employee could scan the tickets. With Roxanne tucked into my side, I led her to the screening room. I did my best to block her view of the giant movie poster outside the screening room, but she saw it. Roxanne gasped, then, with a giddy smile, reached up to kiss my cheek. Her smile reminded me of a kid eating a freshly baked cookie, all warm and excited. *At least I made the right movie choice.* I could feel her vibrating with anticipation.

"You don't know how much I've been wanting to see this movie." She declared.

I led her to our assigned seats. "Oh?"

"My brother and I watched all the Fast and Furious movies together, but he's been so busy with work that we haven't seen this newest one yet."

"Did you want any popcorn?"

"Can't watch a movie without popcorn. Or are you too full?"

I stole a kiss. "I'll be right back."

The snack line was longer than anticipated. By the time I returned, the trailers had already started. I took my seat, offering Roxanne the small popcorn. She took the bag, settled it on her lap and focused her gaze on the screen. I laced my fingers with hers, loving that she didn't pull away. I've never seen any movie in this franchise. About a quarter of the way in, I was as transfixed to the screen as Roxanne.

When the movie ended, I texted my driver to swing by and pick us up. Once in the privacy of the car, I pulled Roxanne onto my lap and devoured her mouth. My need for her was painful. Roxanne shifted into a straddling position and rubbed against me. I ran my hands up the back of her thighs and gripped her ass. She spread her legs and pressed herself closer to me, her fingernails scraping my scalp.

I can't sleep with her, not tonight. Tonight was about proving to her that I'm not a playboy, that I'm not looking for a one-night stand. If I do take her to bed tonight, she may not want a second date. I need a second date. Besides, I doubt she wants me to see the recording device taped to her skin under her dress.

The car arrived at Roxanne's place too soon. I should have had the driver take an extra-long route here. Too late now. With great effort, I forced myself to break the kiss. I removed my hands from under her dress but couldn't bring myself to remove her from my lap.

"You're home." I told her.

"Already?" She pouted.

I chuckled. "Yes, Roxanne, the date is over the moment you leave this car."

"Thank you for tonight." She smiled serenely. "I rather enjoyed myself."

"No need to sound surprised." I teased.

She bit her lip, her cheeks turning pink. "Do you want to come upstairs?"

"Absolutely, but I shouldn't. You're no wham bam, thank you, ma'am."

Roxanne laughed. She slipped her hands inside my jacket to pull out my phone. I unlocked it for her. With deft fingers, she did something and then slid the phone back to where she found it.

Roxanne patted my chest. "Good night, Nico."

I smiled. "Buona notte Bella."

Roxanne smiled, gave me a parting kiss, and then left the car. I felt giddy all the way home. No woman has ever made me feel this way except maybe Rachelle. At the thought of my ex, I frowned. My father will never get his hands on Roxanne. I can't lose her like I lost Rachelle.

Back in my penthouse, I pulled out my phone to see what Roxanne did. I smiled at her saved number. The first thing I did was change her name. Then I called her. She purred into the phone. I hoped she no longer had that listening device because she wouldn't want this conversation recorded. I may not have Roxanne in my bed, but I'll still give her an orgasm to finish the night.

Nine

ROXANNE

"HEY!" I CALLED OUT when I entered my parent's house.

"In the kitchen!" Mom called back.

I removed my shoes at the door, frowning at the extra pair. I then frowned even more profoundly at the additional place setting on the dining room table. My mom was busy mashing potatoes. I kissed her cheek, then took over the mashing job, and she immediately started on a gravy.

"What's with the extra table setting?"

"Jaylen is joining us tonight." Mom answered cheerfully.

"Sundays are supposed to be family nights."

"You know." She hedged with a sly grin. "The two of you would make a cute couple."

I tilted the pot her way. "Is this smooth enough?"

"Yes. Now, that was clear avoidance."

"I'm not avoiding." I countered.

"Yes, you are."

"There are prying ears."

"The men are in the basement." She waved off my concern. "Now talk."

"Mom."

"Roxanne."

I rested my ass against the counter. "What if I told you that Jaylen and I have kind of been seeing each other?"

Mom gave me a knowing grin. "I'd ask you when were you planning on telling me?"

"Can we talk about this in detail later?" I checked her calendar on the fridge. "You have next Tuesday free. Can we do lunch?"

She pursed her lips. "Fine, write it down. We'll talk about this later."

It'll also give me time to figure things out. Nico had called me last night after our date, and the phone sex with him might have been better than the real thing with Jaylen. That could be because I was so wound up from the night that I would have been able to pleasure myself without Nico's voice in my ear. Something about him has me all twisted up in knots.

So, before my lunch date with Mom, I want to figure out how I feel. I thought Jaylen was suitable for me. Now, after the date with Nico, I'm convinced that he's not as advertised. I have to figure it out fast, which is why I'm seeing Lexi later.

"Roxanne." Mom pulled me from my thoughts. "Can you go down and grab the men?"

"Sure."

I kissed her cheek before heading to the basement. Dad used to bring home tough homicide cases to solve them while off the clock. Mom never wanted someone to accidentally walk in and see the gruesome pictures of his cases. So, he built an office space in the basement. When Tyler got older, he'd sneak into Dad's office and read the case files. Quite often, he'd see something that Dad missed and move things around so that when Dad next walked into the office, the solution would be clear as day. I used to help Tyler. I could see the puzzle within the evidence. As I got older, I lost interest, but Tyler continued helping Dad.

I could hear Jaylen, Tyler, and Dad talking. They must have left the door open, or the sound would have been muffled.

"STOP!" Dad bellowed.

I froze on the last step. Listening. I don't want to interrupt them.

"The two of you should have updated me sooner."

"It was last minute." Tyler answered. "We had to move fast."

"The woman Nico went on a date with. You must have known about her sooner."

My heart jumped to my throat. *He can't know it's me.* Dad would kill Tyler for letting me go on a date with Nico, figuratively speaking. He'd probably lock me up for going on a date with Nico. Dad would know Nico as the drug-dealing murderer that Tyler convinced me of on Saturday. That is until I got to know the man.

"Sir." Jaylen interjected. "You know there are too many departments involved in this."

"I'm well aware of that." Dad bit out. "I read your report. The report you handed to me at the end of the day today."

"Let us see where this lead will take us."

"We're trying to convince the woman to help us." Tyler added.

"I want to listen to that recording." Dad demanded.

That can't happen. Dad will recognize my voice. I panicked. Tyler and Jaylen can protect me, but only for a little while.

"There was nothing useful on it." Tyler told him quickly. "You have to trust that we know what we're doing."

I knocked on the wall to announce my presence before taking that last step into the basement. With a smile plastered on my face, I came around the stairs to Dad's office.

"Supper is ready." I announced.

Dad smiled. "Sure thing, sunbeam."

I stepped aside for Tyler and Jaylen to head upstairs. Tyler brushed my hand as he passed. A reassuring gesture. I know he'll do what he can to keep my name out of the investigation and away from Dad. Dad followed his subordinates, pulling me into a hug and kissing my forehead. He closed the door to his office and came up the stairs after me. Mom already had the table full. Bowls and platters of glazed carrots, mashed potatoes, roast beef, popovers, and gravy. We all took a seat and then filled our plates.

"Tell me." Mom began. "Anything new happen this week?"

"I'm sponsoring Dahlia and sending her to Clavus Schola." I informed Mom.

"Who is Dahlia?" Dad asked. "A new employee?"

"Isn't that Carole's niece?" Mom questioned.

"Yep. She has the potential to be great. She needs a little refinement." I answered.

"That's wonderful. I'm sure Carole is thrilled her niece is getting such an opportunity."

I only smiled. *Not a chance.* Carole called me the day after Dahlia handed me the application form. She was pissed that I was taking her niece away. On the other hand, Dahlia's mother had called to thank me for giving her daughter such an opportunity.

"It's been a while since you were last here, Jaylen. Is there anything new with you?" Mom prodded. "Any special woman in your life?"

"There was." Jaylen admitted.

"Was?"

"Her eyes seem to be wandering." His gaze flickered to mine.

"If you believe she's the one, you must prove it to her." Mom advised.

"Jenna, leave the boy alone." Dad sighed. "This woman may not be right for him. Did you run a background check?"

"Herald!"

Mom probably would have hit him if he wasn't at the far end of the table. According to the love story that they told Tyler and me, Dad did a background check on Mom before asking her out. Dad even did one on one of my boyfriends — the one he knew about. He thoroughly approved of the man studying to be a doctor, but it didn't work out. I was dumped because he wanted to focus on his education, then career, and didn't want to string me along. I appreciated his honesty, but it still hurt at the time. There were a few others that Dad didn't know about before I started sleeping with Jaylen, but I figured out on my own that they were no good for me.

"A background check isn't necessary." Jaylen laughed, sending a wink across the table. "I think she might be the one for me."

"That's wonderful." Mom beamed and reached over to squeeze my arm. "Now, how do you plan on getting her back?"

"I've been showing her more affection, but it doesn't seem to be working."

"Let me help you."

"Jenna." Dad interrupted. "Shouldn't you be more concerned over our own children's love life rather than Jaylen's?"

"Don't drag me into this." Tyler pointed to himself. "I'm too busy for anyone. Rox had a date recently."

"Rat." I mumbled.

"A date?" Dad exclaimed. "Who? I need to make sure he's good enough for my sunbeam."

"I'm old enough to figure that out on my own."

"Sure." Tyler snorted.

"I can deal with our children later." Mom interrupted. "Jaylen is like family, and I want to help him with his love life now."

I bit the inside of my cheek to stop myself from laughing. Jaylen's face fell at the mention of being like family, though he quickly recovered when Mom looked back at him. It's a good thing he didn't hear her earlier when she thought he and I would make a cute couple.

I hunkered down over my plate and ate. Mom rattled off suggestions on how Jaylen could get this woman's attention back on him. I suspected he meant me, so I paid close attention. The best way to defend my heart is to know the strategy.

After supper, I helped clean up and put food away before excusing myself. Mom sliced a large chunk of the triple chocolate cake she made for dessert, wrapping it on a plate for me to take to Lexi's. I snatched a bottle of white wine from the basement and headed out the door.

"Finally." Lexi teased when she opened her apartment door to me. "We thought you'd never arrive."

"We?" I questioned, heading to the kitchen.

"Ooo, cake." Barbara took the food from my hand.

"Barb? What are you doing here?"

"I invited her, of course." Lexi stated, pulling wine glasses down from a cabinet. "I know you, Rox. Whatever you say tonight will only be said once. Barb is your oldest best friend, and I'm your more recent best friend. We both deserve to hear about your date."

"Lexi tells me he's hot — like super hot." Barb prodded. "I want to see a picture."

"I don't have a picture." I told them while pouring the wine. "This is perfect. I could use both of your advice."

"I've got the forks." Barb grinned, holding up the utensils.

"I've got the wine." With the bottle in hand, Lexi pointed to the living room. "Off to the couch."

I shook my head, amused by their enthusiasm. With Barbara's hands full with the cake and forks, I took her wine glass. Barb sat in the middle, handed each of us a fork, and dug into the cake. She wiggled in delight.

"Your mom makes the best cake." Barb announced before taking the next bite. "Would she do my wedding cake?"

"You'll have to ask." I shrugged.

"Wedding stuff later." Lexi ordered. "Date stuff now."

With a sigh, I started my tale from the first time Nico Frangione entered my salon. I told them about the kiss in my office, our meet-up at Rocco's and the coffee shop. I was ending the tale with details of the date — including the phone sex. I let them ask all of their questions. Then I went into the Jaylen situation, our friends-with-benefits thing, the out-of-character kisses this past week, and tonight's conversation at my parent's house. I kept my brother's warnings about Nico out of our discussion. They don't need to know about the murder, drugs, and missing women.

"So." I prodded. "That's the full update. I'm not quite sure what to do."

"I still want a picture." Barbara insisted.

"I'm not texting Nico so that you can see what he looks like."

"But I want to know." She wined. "I don't even know what Jaylen looks like."

"That, I can show you."

I pulled my phone out of my back pocket. There are images of Jaylen online that I can show Barbara. Lexi reached over, snatching my phone from my hands so fast my reaction was delayed. She was typing away, doing something I probably wouldn't like. I crawled across Barb's lap. The cake, thankfully, was gone, and the plate sat on the coffee table. Lexi stretched, keeping the phone away from me while Barbara held me down.

"Got it." She declared. "Oh, God, be still my beating heart."

"What?" Barb questioned.

Lexi showed us my phone. "A picture of Nico."

Barb snatched the device and stared. "Damn."

My mouth watered at the picture. Nico held a towel around his waist, his hair wet from a shower as he smirked at the camera. His bare chest revealed muscles and abs one wouldn't think he'd have under his well-tailored suits. A sprinkling of dark hair emphasized the vee that dipped below the towel. There's even a tattoo over his left pec. I couldn't see what it was with the angle at which he held the phone, but I wanted to know. The mischievous glint in his eyes had me snatching my phone back. *He knew exactly what he was doing with this picture.*

"Here's a picture of Jaylen." I eventually said.

I'd pulled up an image of him from a newspaper article written several months ago. It's of him at the children's hospital, lifting them in the air. The joy on both their faces was contagious. The article was about local heroes both in and out of uniform. It also talked about a fireman and nurse who volunteered at an animal shelter. The article adds that the fireman proposed to the nurse while the journalist was there.

"Seriously?" Barbara pouted. "My fiancée is hot, but you have two smoking guys. How is that fair?"

I laughed. "Barb, you have a fiancée. In just a few months, he'll be your husband. These two men might be in my life now, but it means nothing. You at least have a hot doctor locked down."

"Is that what you want?" Barb took my hand. "Someone to be your forever?"

I swallowed hard. "I am a little jealous that you have that, but I'm not about to jump into the deep end just because I want it."

"I understand."

"Why not?" Lexi questioned.

"That's just not me." I shook my head. "I want a relationship, I want love, I want trust. I want what my parents have."

"Do you feel any of that when you're with Jaylen?"

"I feel comfortable with him. There's trust there, but I don't think he wants a relationship. The sex is good, too." I grinned. "I really do like Jaylen. I always have, or else I wouldn't have agreed to a friends-with-benefits."

"What about Nico?" Barbara inquired next.

"He makes me feel tingly and sexy. Like I'm the only woman in the world." I sighed. "The thing about Nico is that he has this playboy aura about him. I fear this charm I'm witnessing will vanish once he successfully gets me into bed. I don't know if he's relationship material."

Barbara covered my eyes with her hand. "I want you to clear your mind of all thoughts and focus on both Jaylen and Nico."

"What for?" I pulled her hand away.

"Just do it." She ordered. "I did this with Jonah after a few dates with him. I wanted to be certain I wasn't getting caught up in a rush of emotions."

"Okay." I indulged her, closing my eyes.

I pulled up an image of both Jaylen and Nico in my mind. I recalled Jaylen's kisses and the look in his eyes when he looks at me. My body relaxed at the thought of him. It's comfortable. Then, I shifted my mind's attention to Nico. Instantly my body felt warm at his cocky smirk and the heat I always seem to see in his eyes. The image of Jaylen faded into the background when I focused on Nico.

"Now tell me, which one do you see more clearly?"

"Nico." I said softly, embarrassed.

"Picture yourself on your wedding day."

My brow furrowed.

"I know you've done that before. I want you to imagine who your groom will be when you walk down that aisle." Barbara slapped her hand over my eyes, stopping me from opening them. "Just do it."

I sucked in a breath, feeling my cheeks burn. "I see Nico."

"Then you take a leap of faith." Lexi told me when I was allowed to open my eyes again. "Go out with Nico again. Give him a chance. You've given Jaylen plenty of time and opportunity. You don't deserve to wait for an idiot who can't see what's right in front of him. You deserve a happy ever after, and Nico could be your prince charming."

"But what if choosing Nico is a bad decision? What if I should have waited for Jaylen?"

"You'll never know." Barbara insisted. "You urged me when I was nervous about going out with Jonah. Now we're planning our wedding. Nico may not be the one for you, but you'll never know unless you give him a chance."

"Besides." Lexi grinned. "If Nico ends up hurting you, I'll beat him to a pulp."

I laughed, leaning forward to hug my two best friends. "I love you both."

"We know."

"Don't forget." Barbara added. "You have to come to my dress fitting in two weeks."

"I know." I reassured her. "And Lexi has the salon booked for your wedding day so the bridal party can have their nails done."

"I talked to a friend of mine." Lexi continued. "She owns a hair salon. When we're done with our nails, we're heading over to her place of business for hair and makeup. She's even coming with us to the chapel and reception to complete touch-ups during the event."

"How much is that going to cost me?" Barb frowned.

"Nothing. This is my bridal gift to you."

"You might have become my new best friend, Lexi."

"Ouch." I feigned hurt. "I'm right here, you know."

Barbara laughed. We spent the next couple of hours talking about wedding stuff before we decided it was time to leave. I'd ignored my phone all night. When I got home, I finally looked at it. There were too many messages from Jaylen. I frowned, dismissing them as I prepared for bed and crawled under the sheets. *I'll deal with Jaylen in the morning.*

Ten

NICO

I TRIED TO STAY focused as Marco led the meeting. He updated the team leads about sale numbers from these past two weeks. He discussed which car in our showroom needs to be pushed. Then he explained the trend he's been seeing with our international team as we track down specific vehicles for our well-paying clientele. When the meeting finished, Marco followed me back to my office, closing the door behind him.

"You're not focused today."

"I can't get that woman out of my head."

"The one that said 'no' to a date with you?" He plopped down in a chair, an amused grin on his lips.

"That's the one." I leaned back in my chair and closed my eyes.

"You need to fuck her out of your system."

"Won't work." I groaned.

"Did you already fuck her?"

I wish. "I took her out for dinner and a movie last night. Then we had phone sex."

Marco let out a low whistle. "Having a case of blue balls?"

I looked at my friend. "She's all I can think about. This isn't good, Marco."

"Okay. You have a few options."

I leaned forward, giving Marco my full attention. He went through this with his now fiancée.

"Opinion one is that you fuck her just to make sure your mind isn't conjuring up a better version than what she actually is. Option two, you could try to scare her away by introducing her to your family." Marco shivered.

"There is no fucking way I'll let her meet my father." I told him sternly.

"Then option one is all you have."

"I may like it too much." I mumbled, defeated.

"I have got to meet this special woman." Marco stood, heading to the door. "To me, it sounds like you've fallen in love."

I stared after Marco. *In love? Impossible.* Love wasn't part of my seduction plan. Besides, people don't fall in love after a single date. There's no way Roxanne could ever love me. There are too many secrets between us — though I know more of hers than she does of mine. Marco's just messing with me. He has to be. Roxanne and I just aren't compatible. I'm only using her to get out of my father's shadow. Once I'm free, then I can let her go. Those words didn't feel right. I can't let Roxanne go.

I spent a couple more hours at work, down on the sales floor. Dealing with walk-in clients was the exact distraction that I needed. I then stopped by Rocco's, hoping the weights might help ease some of my tension. It did — to a point. I no longer felt bodily tense, but it didn't ease my mind at all in regard to Roxanne. On my way home, I swung by a drive-thru for a burger.

Back in the safety of my penthouse, I cracked open a beer and ate my burger. I looked up Roxanne's social media page, curious if she wrote anything about our date. Nothing, but Roxanne did repost Just Yum's post. *Interesting.*

I read the post: You'll have to be satisfied with pictures from the website. It would not have been polite of me to take photos of the food while on a date. What you see is what was placed in front of me. The hype about Croquette is valid. The food was seasoned and cooked to perfection with fresh seasonal ingredients. The small menu allowed the chef to focus on the quality of each dish. Croquette is a date night kind of restaurant. The owners made sure of that. In my sweet tooth opinion, the chocolate soufflé may have been the best thing all night. Now, don't get me wrong, my date was charming, but what man can really compare to a warm, delicious chocolate-baked good?

I smiled. *So, Roxanne writes Just Yum.* Staying anonymous would help her create unbiased reviews. If a restaurant were to figure out that she writes these blogs, they might treat her differently than a regular customer. I finished my burger and continued reading past food blogs. Not all the reviews were positive. What I liked about her negative reviews is that she doesn't diss the restaurant cruelly. She kindly uses wording emphasizing everything is her personal opinion and that her readers may have a different opinion.

Before I knew it, I'd read the entire blog, down to the very first post from three years ago. *I'll have to take Roxanne to other restaurants.* I'd love to read what she thinks about all the restaurants Frostham has to offer that she hasn't tried and take her to other cities and countries for their food options. I'd also love to watch her enjoy the food.

I looked at the time. It was getting late. I hadn't showered after my impromptu stop at Rocco's and decided I should probably do that before going to bed. Just as I stepped out of the shower, my phone pinged with a text from its place on the vanity. The name Bella flashed across the screen, and I couldn't help but smile. It only grew when I read the message.

Bella: This is Lexi, your future girlfriend's loyal guard. It's girls' night, and we need a picture.

Laughing, I complied — after wrapping a towel around my waist. I angled the camera so the picture would get a good view of my body and make Roxanne crave what she could have. Then I went to my room to put on some sweatpants. My phone started to ring. I couldn't stop smiling, thinking it was Roxanne. All amusement faded when I read the caller ID.

"Father." I answered coolly.

"Che cazzo fai Nico?" Straight to the point, not even a simple hello.

"What am I doing? Well, I just finished taking a shower."

"With the Baxter girl." My father ground out. "What the fuck are you doing with her?"

"Baxter girl?" I tried to sound confused.

"Cristo. Don't play dumb with me, Nico. One of my men sent me a picture of the two of you coming out of Croquette last night."

I bit back a curse. I didn't want him to know about Roxanne — at least not yet. *Or maybe at all.* My mind raced to find an explanation to tell him. I couldn't think of one fast enough.

"Well?" Father growled impatiently.

"It was a calculated move." I stalled.

"Spiegare."

I took a deep breath, formulating the lie in my mind. "The plan is to seduce her. She's the weak link in the cop family. I believe I can use her to gather information."

"Being that close to the Baxter's is dangerous." My father's tone lightened with what may have been pride. "I'm impressed you thought of it."

I had to pull the phone away and verify I was talking with my father. I can't remember the last time he praised me. It couldn't be good. He must be making some plan behind my plan — all the more reason to keep Roxanne away from my family.

"Um, thank you?" I said tentatively.

"I'll send Franco in." My father stated. "He'll have the woman wrapped around his finger in no time."

"That's not necessary." I told him, a death grip on the phone.

"Your brother has a way with women."

"I have a rapport with her."

"Your brother will have the information I want within a week."

"I doubt that."

"You doubt your brother's ability with women?" My father laughed. "È altamente qualificato."

"I'm sure women praise Franco's skill in the bedroom." I replied bitterly. "The Baxter girl is different from those in his bed."

"Oh?"

"She'll be suspicious if Franco tries to seduce her now that she's had a date with me. She is the daughter of a cop, after all."

My father grew silent for a moment. "Very well. You have one month to show me your results. If you can't get the job done, then Franco will."

He hung up. I threw the phone onto the bed. *Cazzo!* I bought myself time, but this isn't what I wanted. I can't let Franco anywhere near Roxanne. I'm not exactly sure how she'd react to him. He's a womanizer. Just like our father, he'll fuck anytime, anywhere, and isn't gentle about it. As far as I'm aware, the women he's fucked never seemed to complain.

I sat heavily on the bed and ran a hand through my still-damp hair. I have one month to prove to Roxanne that I want nothing to do with the Frangione business. One month to give my father something to keep Franco away from her. One month isn't enough time. If I don't play my cards right, then Roxanne will walk away with hatred in her heart or get seriously injured. My heart tightened at that thought. Before I see her next, I'm going to have to plan this month very carefully. I won't let what happened to Rachelle also happen to Roxanne.

Eleven

ROXANNE

I GOT OUT OF my car and looked up at the third luxury car dealership Frostham has to offer. *The third time is the charm.* The front half of the building is all glass, showing off the cars inside the structure. The windows let in the sun, which I suspect would keep the inside bright and welcoming. A dark-skinned woman sat behind a crescent-shaped desk. She put down her phone and looked up at me with a smile.

"Welcome to Luxlia Dealers. Do you have an appointment?"

"No." I shook my head. "I'm looking for Nico Frangione."

"Your name?"

"Bella."

She picked up the phone, hit a button, but didn't speak. "He's not in his office." She typed something on her computer. "I've sent him a message that you're here. Do you wish to sit here and wait?"

"Is it okay if I wander the showroom?"

"Of course. I'll let Mr. Frangione know you're on the sales floor."

"Thank you."

I smiled and walked deeper into the dealership. The sun glistened off the cars, making them even more appealing. I looked up. The top floor held more cars. I saw closed doors on the second floor and suspected those were offices. I returned my attention to the vehicles on the first floor. All high-end brands that I'll never be able to afford.

One particular car caught my attention. Deep blue with silver specks in the paint, giving the illusion of a starry night sky. I ran my fingers along the hood to the driver's door. The sleek design made me believe it was a fast car.

"Gorgeous, isn't she?"

I looked up at the voice. A good-looking young man was approaching. He maintained eye contact and a smile. His demeanour screamed salesman. I'm sure he thinks I'll be an easy sale.

"Yes." I agreed.

He came around to open the door. "Have a seat."

"I couldn't."

"I insist."

I really shouldn't. I slid into the seat. The soft, buttery leather was cool even through my clothes. I ran my hands over the steering wheel. I could picture myself driving around the city in this car. *I can't afford this dream.*

"Turn her on." The salesman dangled the keys in front of me. "This baby can purr."

I couldn't resist. I started the car. I could feel the power of the engine vibrate up the seat. I relaxed with a smile. It was a soothing feeling.

"I can take you for a ride." He offered, leaning in the window. "Let you experience a good time."

"I shouldn't." I turned off the engine.

"Trust me. Even if you leave today, you'll be coming back after a ride with me."

"Jacob." A voice scolded. "Let the client look around a bit."

I recognized that voice. *Nico.* Jacob stepped aside moments before the car door opened, and Nico's smiling face greeted me as he helped me out of the car. He took in my appearance: form-fitting denim capri pants and an off-shoulder top. His gaze heated me from the inside out.

"This is a pleasant surprise, Bella." He gave me a chaste kiss.

"Is there someplace we can talk?" I glanced over at Jacob. "Privately?"

"Never a good sign when a woman wants to talk privately." Nico frowned.

"It's important."

"Let's go to my office."

He led me to the second floor, keeping my hand in his. I stepped into the space, taking in my surroundings. The bookshelves lining one wall and the desk are dark, heavy wood.

The oversized and masculine chairs are clad in a deep red fabric. On the opposite wall are a red velvet-looking couch and glass tabletop. The office feels like Nico — dominating, classy, manly. I took in a sharp breath.

"What did you need to talk about?" Nico questioned while closing the door.

I turned to him. My speech, mostly prepared, flew out of my mind at the look in his eyes. Darkened with lust, I shivered at the tendrils of excitement that shot through me. *Focus Roxanne.* I turned my back on Nico, hoping I could say what I needed to communicate better.

"I, uh, well." I stammered.

Am I seriously stammering? I gritted my teeth, hating how nervous I was. I'm supposed to be bold and brave. That's how my dad raised me to be. Yet here I am, uncertain how to ask someone I've gone on a date with once, out for another date. I moved closer to the bookshelf, examining the items on it as I tried to calm my nerves.

"Bella." Nico wrapped his arms around my waist, pulling me into him. "What are you so nervous about?"

"Me? Nervous?" I let out a strangled laugh. "I'm not nervous."

He didn't say anything. He just held me. I found myself relaxing into him. The gesture reassured me that dating Nico is a risk I must take. It could be a bad decision for my heart if what Tyler has warned me of is true, but I may regret never exploring the feeling Nico stirs in me. I ran my hand lightly over a model car he had on display on the bookshelf, ready to tell him why I was there when I felt something I didn't think I should have.

"Where did you get this?"

"My brother." Nico answered coldly.

I pick up the model, bringing it closer to ensure what I feel is what I think it is. *Crap.* Glued onto the hood and painted to look like it's part of the car's design is a listening device. Angling myself in Nico's arms to better show him, I pointed to the device.

"It's interesting." I told him.

Nico frowned. He stared at the model, then stiffened when he realized what I was pointing to. Anger replaced his charming demeanour.

"He gave it to me when I opened this place. He said it'll be good luck."

Nico put the car back on the shelf. He then took my hand and pulled me out of the office, down the hall, and into a new room. This one has an oval table in the center with chairs all around. A boardroom, maybe. A line of windows up high on one wall let in natural light, making the room far more pleasant for long periods.

Nico closed the door and let me go. I stood there watching him walk away from me. His shoulders were stiff, and his hands were fisted at his side. I could feel the dangerous anger rolling off him. It felt darker than an average person's anger. He's pissed, yet I feel no fear of being in danger of this darkness despite him appearing to want to punch something. Nico stopped at a chair, examined it, picked it up and threw it at the wall. I jumped, not expecting the action.

"Nico." I said softly, closing the distance to touch his arm lightly.

"For two years, that car has sat in my office." He turned to me, his eyes black with his anger. "How did you know it was there?"

"I didn't." I told him.

"Roxanne."

I cringed. Hearing him call me by name did something to me. It shouldn't have, but it did. It hurt. I took in a deep breath. *He's hurting.*

"I didn't know it was there." I repeated. "Not until I picked it up."

"How did you know there was something off about the car?"

"I've seen listening devices before. TV shows show them all the time."

Nico stared at me. He weighed my words against his anger for his brother. I stepped even closer, reached up and placed a hand on his cheek. Nico closed his eyes and tilted his head into my hand. My touch calmed his inner beast. Something inside me clicked. Nico needs me. By this simple gesture, I saw how he seemed to find peace with me. Maybe Nico is precisely what I need, too.

Twelve

NICO

A LISTENING DEVICE. IN my office. Planted by my brother. *Cazzo.* I couldn't believe that bastard had snuck a listening device into my office. Yet, it was precisely something Franco would do. Even through my anger, I could feel Roxanne near me. *I won't hurt her.* I refuse to be like Franco or my father. Instead, I threw a chair and accused her of knowing about the listening device, which is ridiculous.

She denied my accusations calmly. Unafraid of my dangerous anger. Roxanne reached up to touch my cheek. I closed my eyes and leaned into her touch. The beast inside was calming at her touch. The warmth she provides fills me, chasing away the darkness that overcame me. I need her.

"Bella."

"That's better." She whispers.

I open my eyes to see her blushing. I want to know why she's blushing. I want to know what she deems as better. As much as I want to know, apologizing feels like the right thing to do.

"I'm sorry." I whisper back.

Roxanne smiled softly. She went up on her toes and left a gentle kiss on my lips. "It's okay."

I'm not sure what to say. This moment feels too... too... vulnerable, like if anything is said, it'll ruin the fragile connection Roxanne and I made. I want to tell her it's not okay, that I shouldn't blame her for anything, and promise her that I'll never hurt her. But words don't come. Instead of speaking, I wrap my arms around her and kiss her. Roxanne opens for me instantly, her arms wrapping around my neck. It feels like it's our first kiss — nothing rushed or lust-filled, just us appreciating each other. Having her in my arms feels right.

Roxanne moved her hands to my shoulders and pushed me back gently. "We still need to talk."

"About what?" I asked, resting my forehead against hers.

"Well, us, actually." She pushed and took a step out of my arms. "I, uh. If you want, um. I was wondering if."

Roxanne stammered and twisted her hands together. I stood there patiently waiting for her to continue. I wanted to hold her but sensed she needed space to think. Whatever she had to say, she was clearly nervous about my reaction. She bit her bottom lip as if deciding her next words. I saw the moment her words were chosen.

She took a deep breath and looked me straight in the eye. "I want to go on another date."

A slow smile curved my lips. *Absolutely.* I opened my mouth to answer when she held up her hand.

"Before you say anything, you need to know something. My brother is a cop, and I wore a listening device on our first date."

I knew all this already. She watched me, waiting for an answer. I could use this moment in my favour.

"Bella." I took her hands in mine. "The cops have been following me for the past month. If going on a date with me puts you in an awkward position, I'm sorry."

Her brows knitted together. Her pursed lips told me she knew already. *I wonder what her brother has divulged.* When it was clear that she wasn't going to say anything, I continued.

"They clearly want something. If they told you to date me so they can collect evidence against me for some crime they believe I've committed, then I'm going to have to turn down your request for a second date."

I hoped she denied that statement. I really want a second date. Roxanne stared at me for a beat before bursting out with laughter. I frowned. *What is so funny?* When she finally calmed, Roxanne smiled.

"My brother did ask me to be his inside woman, but I turned him down."

"I don't understand."

"I'm here." She stepped closer. "Because my two best friends made me realize that I should give you a chance. I'm here not for the police but for myself." Bella blushed. "I want to date you because you make me feel important and sexy."

My heart seized. I'm supposed to be using this woman. She wasn't supposed to fall for me that quickly. I wanted her to keep some walls up against me. Instead, she tore them down to give me a chance.

"Roxanne." I started.

She grimaced.

"What?"

"It doesn't sound right when you say my name." Her blush deepened. "I much prefer Bella."

I smiled, cupping her cheek. "Bella Baxter, you are the most intriguing woman I've met in years. I would love to take you out on another date."

"Why does it sound like there's a 'but' coming?"

"This Saturday, my niece and nephew will be having their seventh birthday party. Will you come as my date?"

"Meet your family?"

"Extended family." I augmented. "Cousins, aunts, uncles. My brother and father will not be there."

Roxanne bit her bottom lip, contemplating. "Okay."

"Okay? Really?" I questioned cautiously.

"Yes, really."

"Okay. I'll pick you up at one. It's a backyard BBQ, so there's no need to dress to impress." I grinned. "Unless you want to impress me."

She smiled, wrapping her arms around my neck. "Impressing you shouldn't be too difficult."

"I'm not so sure." I wrapped my arms around her waist, pulling her against my body and brushed my lips against hers. "I have high standards."

My phone buzzed with a text message, breaking our moment. I pulled back to read it. A frown formed on my lips. Marco sent me a warning that he saw Franco in the lobby. *What does he want?*

"Cazzo." I cursed out loud.

"What's wrong?" Roxanne inquired.

"An unwanted meeting just walked into the building."

"Okay." She gave me a soft kiss. "I'll see you Saturday."

That's it? She didn't pout or whine about me needing to go. It was odd. The women I used to sleep with tried to keep me around longer. Not Roxanne. She was already heading to the door. It was refreshing.

"Wait." I panicked. I was pulling her back before she could step out into the hall. I looked around to ensure Franco wasn't there. "Take the elevator down."

She looked like she wanted to argue. Roxanne, thankfully, nodded. I watched her enter the elevator before turning and heading to my office. Franco was letting himself in when I turned the corner. If Roxanne had come this way, they would have definitely crossed paths. I took a couple of steadying breaths and straightened my suit before walking in.

"Franco." I said blandly.

My brother was already sitting on the couch, an arm over the back and an easy grin on his face. So many women think he's charming. *Roxanne wouldn't, would she?* Franco didn't move.

Instead, he signalled for me to take a seat, as if this is his office and I'm the guest. I chose to stay standing, arms crossed and glaring. It can't be a coincidence that Franco showed up in my office now while Roxanne was in the building.

"Nico." He sounded cheerful.

"What are you doing here?"

"I wanted to check in on my little brother."

I scoffed. "I doubt that. You're here for business. So, what is it?"

Franco leaned forward, resting his elbows on his knees. "Father told me of your plan with the Baxter woman."

"It's none of your business."

"Actually, it is. You're putting the whole family at risk."

"Father approves."

"I looked into her." A dark smile curled his lips. "She's far too much of a woman for you to handle."

I gritted my teeth and clenched my hands into fists. *There's no fucking way Franco is going near Roxanne.* It took all my willpower not to fly across the room and punch my brother. *Roxanne is mine.* That thought is the only thing that kept me in place. She came to me asking for another date. She told me about her brother being a cop. She's giving me a chance.

"Bastardo." I mumbled, then more clearly said. "She'll only shoot you down."

"I can be very charming."

"She's not like the other women you've been with."

He shrugged. "You've been out of the game too long. Showing women a good time is my specialty."

"I'm not going to make this a competition." I growled.

"Father may think you'll come through." Franco stood. "I have my doubts, little brother."

With that ominous threat, he left. Feeling like my knees were about to buckle, I took a seat on the couch he just vacated. *What the fuck am I going to do?* I repositioned myself so I was lying down and covered my eyes with an arm. If Franco does go after Roxanne, there's a slim possibility that she'll fall to his charms. If I warn Roxanne of his potential advances, then I'll be at risk of revealing the lie I told my father about using her to gather information about my family. This has turned into a big mess.

"Nico?"

I heard Paige call softly from the door. I ignored her. Undeterred, she entered my office. I heard the door click shut and her heels click across the floor to me. I didn't move. The couch shifted, and I felt a weight come down on me.

I pulled my arm away to see Paige straddling my lap. "What are you doing?"

"Helping you relax." Paige purred, grinding her hips into mine.

"No."

I sat up. Taking hold of her hips, I lifted her off my lap and settled her on the couch. Not wanting her anywhere near me, I stood and went to the door. Did I not make myself clear enough last time?

"You should get back to work, Paige."

She frowned, her brows furrowing in confusion. "I'm only trying to help."

"Get out of my office. I'm not going to fuck you."

I know my tone was much harsher than it should have been. I want nothing to do with her, and I have to make myself clear now. Just before she left, she reminded me that I could call on her at any time. *That is not going to happen.* I need to double my efforts with Roxanne, and fucking an employee isn't the way to go.

Thirteen

ROXANNE

It was a busy morning. Even Candi and Brina walked in. There was no drama this time, thankfully. Having finished with my morning clients, I returned to my office to grab my purse. Then, I returned to the front to let Lexi know that I was heading out.

"Going to see Nico?" Lexi questioned.

I shook my head. "I hope to get a bite before my afternoon clients come in."

Lexi tapped her pen rhythmically on the counter. "What was that with Candi?"

"You'll have to be more specific."

"Does she know?" She leaned forward, lowering her voice. "That you and her brother? I mean, she was rather respectful today."

"I don't think so." I pondered.

My cell phone rang. Nico's personalized ringtone: I'm too sexy. I smiled, and Lexi laughed. The ringtone suits him perfectly.

"Hello?" I questioned playfully. "Who might this be?"

"Bella." Nico's deep voice rumbled through the phone.

"I'm sorry, I don't know anyone by that name."

He laughed. My smile widened. *He has such a nice laugh.* I should make a point of getting him to laugh more often.

"What can I do for you, Nico?"

"Join me for lunch." He suggested.

"I would love —."

My acceptance fell flat as Jaylen walked into my salon. *What is going on?* Jaylen has never shown up unannounced before. I don't think he's ever just shown up at my salon before. *Did something happen to Tyler? Or dad?* My heart rate picked up. Nico called my name, and I gave a little jump. I forgot I was on the phone with Nico.

"Hold that thought." I told Nico. Moving the phone to my shoulder, I spoke directly to Jaylen. "What are you doing here?"

"You've been ignoring my calls." He stated. "So, I thought I'd stop by and invite you to lunch."

"Lunch?" I repeated dumbfounded.

"Yes, lunch. I know you like going to Sandis. Let me take you."

I looked at Lexi, but she only shrugged. We were both stunned by his request. This is unusual. I wondered what he wanted. I shouldn't even contemplate having lunch with him. Curiosity, though, won over.

"Fine. We need to talk anyway." I put the phone back to my ear. "Something personal just came up. I'll talk to you later."

"Is everything okay?" Concern laced Nico's voice.

"Yeah, it will be. Trust me."

"I do, Bella. I'll hold you to that phone call later."

"I'm sure you will." I hung reluctantly up. "Okay, Jaylen, shall we?"

"Yes." He perked up. Turning around, he opened the door for me. "After you."

I stepped out onto the sidewalk. Jaylen placed a hand on my lower back. I resisted the urge to step away. Now that my mind's made up, his touch didn't elicit the same feeling as Nico's touch does. Sandis is a sandwich shop just down the street from Dagger Designs. It was busy, as it usually is around lunch. We waited for a table.

"How has your day been?" Jaylen asked casually when we were seated several minutes later.

"Fine." I frowned at him. "What are you doing, Jaylen?"

"Having a conversation and going to enjoy a meal with a beautiful woman."

The compliment didn't sound right. Not from him. *He wants something.* The first time Jaylen complimented me, we fell into bed together, and he convinced me of a friends-with-benefits relationship. The next time he complimented me, he convinced me to be his plus one to an out-of-town wedding for a high school friend. By the third time, I caught on that his compliments were a way to soften me up for a request. I didn't mind since I wanted to be with Jaylen, but it would have been nice to hear them more often.

The waitress came around to collect our order. I ordered the pear and brie panini with cream of cheddar broccoli soup. Jaylen ordered a classic grilled cheese with tomato basil soup. She wandered away, leaving us alone again.

"It's not like you to ask me out for lunch out of the blue." I started. "The few times we've had lunch together, it was planned. We've either had takeout in my office, where you snuck in through the back door. Or I'd meet you somewhere for a private lunch."

"I thought it was about time I changed my ways."

"Why?"

"Because you deserve more than what I've been giving you." He said earnestly.

That was unexpected. I stared at Jaylen, uncertain how to respond. I'm unsure if he's serious or just leading to his grand request. I steeled myself for either route. Before Jaylen suggested the friends-with-benefits, I'd been crushing on him, and my feelings grew over the year we'd been sleeping together. Then Nico blew into my life.

"I don't understand." I admitted.

The conversation halted when the food was placed in front of us. Sandis has always been quick service. The silence continued as we began eating. In the quiet, I began to recall all the suggestions Mom had given Jaylen on Sunday, ways to get the woman he wanted back. Complimenting her and being honest was part of that list, along with the suggestion to surprise her.

"I realized something recently." Jaylen started the conversation back up. "Something I should have realized a lot sooner."

I braced myself. "Which is?"

"How much I want you."

I froze with my next bite halfway to my mouth. I stared at Jaylen. A swirl of mixed emotions clouded my mind — shock and excitement over his declaration. Also, I was guilty that I was planning to break off whatever we had. All the emotion got caught in my throat. I also felt hurt that he's waited this long to say anything. There was hope in Jaylen's eyes as he watched me. *Does he think I'll swoon at his confession?*

I took a bite, swallowing before speaking. "You want me?"

"Yes."

"And you only realized this now? What changed?"

"Nico Frangione." He confessed. "Since you met him, I knew you could be in danger. I also knew I could lose you, and I couldn't let that happen. I didn't realize right away that I didn't want you to go out with him because I wanted you to be mine. It wasn't until I heard you flirting with him that I realized how much you mean to me. I think, though, subconsciously, I knew I wanted you even before Nico came into the picture."

"The flirting was all to put him at ease around me." I lied.

"I know." He stated with a nod. "I'm sure the kissing was all part of that plan, too."

I flushed, embarrassed that all of it was caught on tape. A tape that my dad wants to hear. *Did he listen to it? Or has Ty somehow been able to keep my involvement under wraps?* Jaylen reached across the table and took my hand.

"After your fake date, I noticed you were distant toward me. I was afraid he'd gotten under your skin. Ty is the one who pointed out my pissy mood. Then, what Jenna said at dinner the other day shifted things into perspective for me. It wasn't until I learned that you went to Nico's car dealership yesterday that I realized exactly how much I want you. How much I need you. Seeing you with another man, even just hearing about it, made me jealous."

"Jealous?" I repeated.

"Jealous." He agreed. "You weren't, aren't, mine. I want you to be. I want to be the only man in the world to make you smile like no one else can. I want to be the only man you crave to have at night."

My throat went dry. *Why now?* These are all the right words. The right words I would have fawned over if he had said them before Nico came into the picture. Jaylen laced his fingers with mine. I stared at them. Everything inside wared with each other. My head told me to step away, but my heart urged me to go after the man I'd been wanting for the past year.

"Roxanne, I want to be yours." He said softly.

I looked up at him. He pleaded with his eyes to give him a chance to redeem himself. I pulled my hand back and reached for my water. This confession has come too late. I already came to that decision. I agreed to lunch with Jaylen to tell him to his face that I needed to let him go. Jaylen took too long. Nico has shown he's interested, so I'm choosing to be with him. Jaylen's confession only makes things more challenging. I might have said yes without hesitation if he had said any of these things Sunday before I went to Lexi's. Or better yet, weeks or even months ago.

"No." I told him.

The word came out quietly, getting stuck in my throat. I pushed my empty plate away. I need to get out of here. I fished out more than enough cash to cover my meal without looking at the bill and left Sandis. I could hear Jaylen scramble to leave money on the table and follow. The sun shone brightly outside — completely contrasting how I felt inside. I raised my arm to block the blinding light before turning away and returning to work.

"Roxanne, wait." Jaylen caught my elbow.

"No." I pulled my arm back and kept walking.

Jaylen skipped ahead to block my path. "Rox, talk to me."

I squared my shoulders and looked him in the eye. "We, no, I am ending our friends–with–benefits arrangement."

A slow smile began to form on his lips. I shook my head. Jaylen's smile faded, a look of confusion now on his face.

"That date with Nico had me realizing something too." I told him. "I want a relationship. I want someone to want me, for me."

"That's what I'm offering, a relationship." Jaylen countered.

"No." I shook my head again. "You're just saying the words you think I want to hear because you want to keep me in your bed. I want to end it, Jaylen."

"That's not true." He shifted. "Well, yes, I want to keep you in my bed, but that's only part of it."

"I want to date and find someone I can picture myself with at the altar."

"I can be that person, Roxanne. I want to be that someone. I want to be the one you see in the morning and go to bed with at night. I want to be that plus one to events and the one you go to when your day is bad."

"You've had me for a year, Jaylen. I've given you all of that. You didn't want more than what was on the surface." I took a steadying breath. "Your confession of wanting more has come too late. You waited too long. I need more, and I don't think you can provide it."

"I can." Jaylen took hold of my arms. "I can be anything you need. Just let me prove it to you. I am ready."

I pushed his arms away and side-stepped him. *This is too much.* I didn't expect separating myself from Jaylen would be this difficult. It wouldn't have been this hard if he didn't confess to wanting a relationship. I'm going to need a few minutes alone in my office to collect myself. I looked at the time on my phone. There's not enough time between now and my afternoon client to call Nico. Instead, I sent him a text.

Me: Can we meet up tonight?

Nico: Of course. Is everything okay?

Me: Yes.

Me: No.

Nico: Bella?

Me: I don't know.

Nico: Call me when you're done work. We can talk while you drive home. I'll meet you there.

Me: Thank you.

It wasn't much, but that short conversation made me feel better. I wiped my eyes and checked my appearance in the washroom, then went onto the salon floor for my next client.

Fourteen

NICO

INVITING ROXANNE TO MY niece and nephew's birthday reminded me that I haven't heard from Tina's Toys about their gifts. By the time I finished work yesterday, the store was closed, so I figured a quick stop in the morning wouldn't hurt. My dealership can run without me, but I like going in. I'm proud of the business I created without any help from the family.

Tina's Toys is located near the largest mall Frostham has to offer, just on the edge of the downtown area. This particular toy store not only sells mass-market toys but can also customize toys. They have a whole team in the back that can do that, whether it's simply taking a toy off the shelf and customizing the outfit or building a new, unique toy for the child.

I've become a regular customer. I have always provided a unique toy to my niece and nephew. Gina — the owner — claims to love seeing my orders as they give her team a challenge. She inherited the business from her parents, who had inherited it from her grandparents. Gina added to the successful toy store by adding the customization area. She's even partnered with Build-a-Bear to have a corner just for them.

"Nico." Gina beamed when I found her stocking a shelf of Batman toys. "I was going to call you today."

"The toys are done?"

"I think your niece and nephew are going to love them." She said excitedly. "Come, I'll show you."

Gina abandoned the mass market toys. I followed the petit blonde to the back, past the employee-only sign. She opened a door with the sign that said: Magic Happens Here. It revealed the workshop. Half a dozen workers were busy customizing customer orders. Gina led me through the room and stopped in front of a car and kitchen set.

"One realistic kitchen for your niece and one miniaturized Corvette C8 for your nephew." Gina beamed. "Both electric and fully functioning."

"Sorprendente." I opened the car door. "It looks exactly like the real thing."

"The power supply is in the gas tank area. One night of charge and the car will run for eight hours."

"What about the kitchen?"

"It'll have to be plugged into the wall to work. The microwave, stove, and oven are all electric. It is the replica of the one from the pictures you gave us."

"È perfetto."

"Now that I have your seal of approval, I'll have the toys delivered this afternoon."

"Actually, can you hold off until Saturday?" I inquired. "It'll be difficult to keep these hidden from Annabelle and Toni."

Gina laughed. "Let me check the delivery schedule."

I followed Gina to her office on the second floor. The walls were covered with large print copies of every month for the year — the dates filled in for when customized orders were due. Gina sat at her desk, typing away. I examined some design plans she also had posted on her walls. Before inheriting the toy store, Gina went to school for mechanical engineering, and this toy store lets her explore and experiment in her field of study.

"I can have the car and the kitchen delivered for three o'clock Saturday afternoon." Gina announced.

"Perfect. I'll let Sonia and Oliver know."

"Do you know what you want for Christmas?"

Roxanne, at my side. I thought.

"One event at a time." I told Gina. "Christmas is still five months away, and it's only June."

"You know how busy we get in December." She gestured to the wall of calendars. "December is already half full."

"I know." I assured her. "Give me a little time to think it over. It has to be perfect, so I stay the favourite uncle."

"Of course." She teased. "We wouldn't want you dropping in rank."

Gina walked me out. I started to drive toward work when I glanced at the clock. The morning went by fast. I smiled to myself, picturing Roxanne's smiling face if I stopped by to take her for lunch. Then, the cop car following me caught my eye in the rearview mirror. It'll probably be better if I call first, then I can meet her somewhere.

I pushed a button on the steering wheel. "Call Bella."

The call went through. I listened as it rang once, twice, then three times. She might still be working and unable to pick up.

"Hello?" Roxanne answered, a smile in her voice. "Who might this be?"

"Bella."

"I'm sorry, I don't know anyone by that name."

I laughed. *Smartass.* I really wanted to kiss her. I restrained myself from stepping on the gas pedal to get to her salon faster.

"What can I do for you Nico?" She asked.

"Join me for lunch."

It's not quite a demand and not posed as a question. I want her to say yes. I want to see her.

"I would love —." Her sentence fell away.

There was silence on the other line. Concerned, I called out to her.

"Hold that thought." She said.

I could hear the phone moving away from her mouth. There were some muffled voices: a man's and Roxanne's. The cheerful tone she used with me didn't sound like it had stayed.

"Something personal just came up." Roxanne told me. "I'll talk to you later."

"Is everything okay?" I asked, concerned.

"Yeah, it will be. Trust me." Her words sounded forced.

"I do, Bella. I'll hold you to that phone later."

"I'm sure you will."

Roxanne hung up on me. Whatever personal matter had come up did not please her. Or that could be wishful thinking on my part. I turned the corner, her salon just up ahead. I saw Roxanne exit with some brown-haired male. It wasn't her brother, he had blond hair. The guy placed his hand on her lower back, walking down the street with her. I looked in the rearview at them as I passed. He seemed pleased to be with Roxanne. I was so focused on the guy that I didn't even look to see Roxanne's expression.

Roxanne is mine. I gripped the steering wheel tightly. It took all my willpower to keep driving. If I pulled over now to break his hand for touching her, Roxanne might change her mind about dating me. She wants to give me a chance. If I react out of possessiveness, she may not want to give me that chance. *I can't fuck up with her.* Roxanne has me feeling things I haven't felt in years. It hit me hard and fast, and I refuse to let go of these feelings.

I steered the car toward Royal Heights, the wealthiest area of Frostham. The houses and properties are massive. They were gated off from the road for privacy. The Frangione house is out here. So is Oliver and Sonia's house. I pulled up to the gate and punched in the code for the gates to open. Aside from the couple hours in the afternoon spent at Croquette, my cousin and his wife are usually home. Typically, their kids would be in private school, the best money can afford, but it's summertime.

The gate code is handed out to a select few people. Because so few people have the gate code, they never bother with locking the front door if they are home.

"Oliver? Sonia?" I called out after entering.

"In the kitchen." Sonia replied, smiling when she saw me. "Nico, this is a pleasant surprise."

I kissed her cheek. "I just wanted to let you know I'm having Toni and Annabelle's gift delivered Saturday at three."

She frowned. "You didn't have to come all the way here to tell us that."

"Nico." Oliver walked in from the patio. "I wasn't expecting to see you until Saturday."

"And you will." I assured him. "I hope you don't mind if I bring someone."

Sonia squealed. "Is this the woman you brought to Croquette?"

I nodded.

"I can't wait to meet her."

Oliver washed his hands. "Join us for lunch."

"Grazie. Where are the kids?" I inquired while going to the fridge to pull out the jug of iced tea Sonia always has stored inside.

"In the pool. They'll be joining us as soon as they dry off."

Oliver set out an extra place setting for me at the table. At the same time, Sonia pulled out two pizzas from the oven and began slicing. Toni and Annabelle came barrelling into the dining room from outside. Their towel-clad bodies raced for a hug from their favourite uncle.

Once seated, the five of us ate lunch. My niece and nephew excitedly told me about their birthday plans. They dominated the conversation. After lunch, Sonia told them to put on some clothes, and then they could watch a movie while we adults talked. There was some whining, but Oliver sternly told them to listen to their mother. One final hug from me, and they were off.

"So." Sonia prompted. "What is this woman like?"

"Lei è perfectta." I couldn't stop the smile forming on my face. "Beautiful, intelligent, a businesswoman, but there are some complications."

"Oh?"

I gave them a brief recap of events. Starting with her connection with the cops, my father's interest, our date, and Roxanne's confession to provide me with a shot. My cousin and his wife listened carefully. I helped to clear the table as I talked. I didn't leave anything out. I even told them what I saw coming here and how I felt seeing someone else touch Roxanne.

"Definitely some complications." Oliver agreed. "I'd be concerned when Roxanne's father, Captain Baxter, learns of your involvement in his daughter's life. The brother sounds overprotective, and that's probably mild compared to her father."

I groaned. For all I know, fake evidence could be planted so that I'd be arrested and pulled away from Roxanne. Her father could quite possibly be able to convince Roxanne that I'm too dangerous of a criminal. I don't know how far Captain Baxter will go to protect his daughter or how far he'll go to put my family in jail.

"Is Roxanne worth all the complications?" Sonia asked me earnestly.

"Yes." I answered without hesitation, returning to the table. "I haven't felt this way about anyone. Not even my feelings for Rachelle can compare."

Her brows rose in surprise. "Really?"

"I loved Rachelle, but she left me."

"After meeting your father." Oliver reminded me.

"Yeah." I agreed solemnly. "But I didn't go after her, and I didn't protect her."

"She wasn't the one, or you would have followed her." Sonia placed three sorbets on the table and sat down. "If the past repeated, would you go after Roxanne?"

"In a heartbeat. I'm doing everything I can to keep her away from my father."

Oliver snorted. "Enzo Frangione will insist on meeting the woman his son is dating. Even if he uses that as a pretense."

"I think the best way to protect Roxanne is to tell her the truth." Sonia said. "Tell her what your father wants before she finds out some other way."

"What good will that do?" I questioned.

"You could lose her if you don't. It sounds like she's taking a big chance on you, Nico. If you screw up, it'll break her, she'll know she made a bad decision, and she'll want nothing to do with you. Trust me."

"You remember Jackie?" Oliver cut in.

"You're manipulative ex?" I confirmed though I'm not sure why he brought her up. "How can I forget?"

"I had recently broken up with Jackie again, and I swore I'd never get back together with her." Oliver began. "That's when I went to a diner and saw the most beautiful angel. I was so taken by her beauty that I impulsively asked her out. Of course, she said no."

"Oliver came back to the diner every day that week to ask me out." Sonia continued. "Annoyed, I accepted. I figured I could indulge him this once, then he'll move on."

"I took Sonia to an event where I could meet restaurant owners and chefs. This was when I started getting the idea to open Croquette, but I wasn't sure how to go about it. My father's money could only get me so far. I needed Sonia to be my arm candy for the night. If I went alone, I was sure to be bombarded by any single woman present." Oliver took his wife's hand. "I learned a lot about Sonia that night and found myself more interested in her than in starting my own restaurant."

"The night was enjoyable until I bumped into Jackie in the washroom." Sonia's nose scrunched. "She told me Oliver was only using me to make her jealous. The thought of being used like that hurt, and knowing this night was a big deal to him, I didn't confront Oliver until he was parked in front of my house."

I was leaning forward intently. Oliver has never told me the whole story of how he and Sonia got together. I knew he saw her working at a diner, asked her out, fell in love, and the rest is history.

"I was so surprised when she asked if I was using her." Oliver chuckled. "Since I didn't deny it, she got out of the car, slammed the door and stomped into her house. At the time, I thought she meant as arm candy, not as a jealousy game."

"I had fallen for Oliver that night. Hurt by his actions, I switched my shifts at work and blocked his number."

"I gave her a week to cool off before I tried to reach out again — with no luck. Jackie came sauntering back. When I denied her, she asked if the whore I used had gotten to me. That might have been the first time I ever saw red. I only then realized what Sonia meant when she asked me if I was using her. That night, I went after her. Sonia wasn't at the diner, she wasn't picking up her phone, and she wasn't answering her front door. I was just about ready to kick it in when she answered. As angry as she was, I still found her beautiful."

I looked at Sonia. "Did you chew him out before slamming the door in his face?"

Oliver laughed. "I didn't give her a chance."

"He kissed me senseless, then took me to bed." Sonia explained, laughing herself. "Eventually, he cleared up the misunderstanding. I was still insulted that he'd used me as arm candy, so I kicked him out in the morning."

"This angelo of mine didn't make it easy for me, but she let me do everything to apologize." Oliver finished.

"Wow." That was all I could say. "Your story is a little more complex than you've let on."

"The point." Sonia looked pointedly at me. "Is that the longer you wait to tell Roxanne the truth, the harder it'll be for you to get her back when she leaves. And she will leave. She sounds independent enough not to be listening to any warnings her family is clearly giving her, but she will go to them if they end up being right."

I grimaced. "How am I supposed to tell her the truth? I asked her out because I wanted to use her to get out of my father's shadow. Prove to the family that I want nothing to do with them. Yet, my father found out about our date and wants me to use her to gather information."

"Which you suggested." Oliver reminded me.

"He had no choice." Sonia winced. "Whatever you tell her, you'll have to be tactful in your truth."

"She must be smart." Oliver stated. "She'll understand. Just don't wait too long. The sooner, the better."

They could be right. I have to figure out how to make her understand that I want her, for her, before I drop the bombshell of my father's demands. Franco's threat still lingered in my mind, too. If he gets to Roxanne before I get a chance to talk to her, he could fuck up everything. I let out a heavy sigh. It doesn't matter what I do, whether it's keeping things from Roxanne or telling her everything. Her reaction is only going to be negative, and I'll probably lose the only good thing that's in my life right now.

Roxanne's text came as I was leaving Oliver and Sonia's. She sounded upset. I wanted to go to her now, but she wanted me over tonight. I'm uncertain if this is a good thing or a bad thing.

I talked to Roxanne until she got home. I arrived a few minutes before she did and waited outside her apartment door. When Roxanne arrived, she ended the call and rushed into my arms. She looked like she had cried today. I took her keys, unlocking her apartment. I carried her in, locked the door, and went to the couch. Roxanne kept her face buried in my chest as I rubbed her back.

"Do you want to talk about it?" I asked gently.

"No." She mumbled. "Yes."

"Whenever you're ready."

"Someone said something to me today." Roxanne said. "I thought it was something I wanted to hear."

I didn't understand what she was talking about. I don't think she was expecting me to answer. So, I sat there with Roxanne in my lap and rubbed her back. She wasn't crying. She just wanted to be comforted. It's a role I'm unfamiliar with, but for Roxanne, I'll learn to be whatever she needs.

"That made no sense." She admitted, raising her head. "Before you, I was in a friends–with–benefits relationship."

My arms tightened around her. *Could that have been the guy she had lunch with?* Roxanne smiled softly, trailing her fingers along my jaw, then she kissed my nose.

"I broke it off with him today. Except, he confessed how much he wanted me."

Her earlier words sunk in. I swallowed hard before asking. "You wanted him to confess."

"I did, but he was too late."

"So, you won't be sleeping with him anymore?"

"No. I'm loyal in my relationship, even if all we're doing is dating."

I kissed her hard. My guilt nearly overshadowed the joy I felt over confession. I need to tell her the truth soon, maybe after the BBQ on Saturday.

Fifteen

ROXANNE

I'D CHANGED MY OUTFIT three times before there was a knock on my apartment door. I looked at the alarm clock next to my bed. *Nico's early.* I went to answer the door and could only stare slack-jawed at the man. He wore the most casual outfit I've seen him in to date. Khaki-coloured shorts and a navy blue t-shirt, he looks delicious.

"Ready to go?"

I shook my head. "I just need to change and grab my purse."

"Change? What for?" Nico grabbed my hand and pulled me to him. "You look beautiful."

"The shorts might be too short."

Nico kissed me. His hands ran up the back of my thighs and squeezed my ass cheek. He pressed me into him so I could feel what my outfit was doing to him. With a little moan, I wrapped my arms around his neck loosely.

"Nope, not too short." He said against my lips before kissing me again.

He lifted my leg to hook around his waist and stepped into my apartment. His kiss set me on fire. I felt something at my back and pulled my mouth away from his. Nico kissed along my jaw and down my neck.

"Let me grab my purse." I said breathlessly. "Then we can go to the BBQ."

Nico groaned, reluctantly letting me go. Returning to my bedroom, I grabbed a cropped blouse, slipped it over my red spaghetti strap top, and tied the ends under my breasts. The long-chained clutch sat on my bed, ready to go with my phone, keys and ID. Returning to the front door, Nico held the door open for me. I slipped into wedge-heel sandals, bending down to fasten them around my ankles, and then locked my apartment behind me.

"Wait a minute." I unlocked the door and rushed to the coffee table to grab the two gift bags sitting there. "Can't forget these."

Nico frowned at the bags. "You didn't have to get anything."

"I can't just arrive at the birthday party empty-handed."

"It'll make more of an impression on Oliver and Sonia than it will on Toni and Annabelle."

With my apartment locked up once more, Nico put an arm around my waist and walked me to his car. He opened the passenger door for me, taking the gifts to put in the trunk before sliding behind the wheel. I ran my hands over the soft leather seat. *Nico likes his luxury.*

"No chauffeur this time?" I teased.

"That was for a special occasion." He winked. "I wanted to impress you."

"I was more impressed that you actually had reservations for Croquette."

Nico laughed. "I hope to impress you every time we're together, Bella."

I shifted in my seat. The words were innocent enough, but they didn't feel innocent. They felt like they were a promise for so much more. Jaylen always treated me with respect. Nico does, too, but he also makes me feel like a desirable woman. Jaylen's words and actions felt almost generic compared to Nico's words and actions. *I have to stop. Jaylen doesn't matter now.*

"Bella, did you tell anyone about today?" Nico asked.

"Lexi knows I have a date with you. Why?"

"The blue sedan, two back, has been following us since I left your apartment."

I looked out the back window. "Make a left turn so I can get a look at the driver."

Nico followed my request. Jaylen was following us. *Why is he following us?* I pulled my phone out, turned off the location, and turned the device off. I rummaged through the glovebox for something to use to pop the SIM card out of my phone. Finding a paperclip, I used that. Now, no one will be able to trace me.

"I recognize him." I told Nico. "He's my brother's partner."

"Hold on, Bella, I'll lose the tail."

Nico shifted gears and sped up. He went through yellow lights and turned corners without signalling. The drivers of Frostham weren't too impressed. A few honks echoed behind us, but he wasn't doing anything that would warrant being pulled over. Besides, being pulled over would break Jaylen's cover. Eventually, he lost Jaylen's tail. I felt a sense of relief over losing the tail.

I reached over, squeezing Nico's leg. "That was hot."

"How hot?" Nico questioned playfully.

"I've never been in a car chase before."

"That wasn't exactly a car chase, Bella."

"Doesn't matter. The speed was exhilarating."

"Duly noted."

Nico picked up my hand, kissing the palm. My breath caught on the intimate action. Keeping my hand in his, he drove out to Royal Heights. Pulling up to one of the many gated mansions, he punched in the code that opened the gates. I slid forward to gawk out the front window. The gorgeous colonial-style house was something out of movies or magazines. White siding, blue shutters, pillars by the door holding up an awning, and a meticulously maintained garden.

"Despite the house, the owners are not stuck up." Nico chuckled.

"This place is breathtaking."

"Would you want to live in a house like this?"

I shook my head. "Too big for one person."

"What if you had a husband and children?"

I glanced at Nico. I was tempted to tease him, ask if he'd fulfill the role of husband, but I couldn't get the words past the lump in my throat. The image it invoked did something to my insides, something I don't want to examine right now. Realizing he was watching me intently, waiting for an answer, I shook my head again.

"The house is still too big."

Nico nodded. "What kind of house could you picture yourself living in?"

"Something a little bigger than what you see in the suburbs. My dream home would be big enough for two kids and a dog, private enough for them to run around yet still have neighbours. The rooms would be large enough to entertain without being extravagant. I'd want to customize the kitchen, and the most important thing would be a soaker tub in my ensuite bathroom. Something for me to relax in at the end of a long day, either by myself or with my husband." I looked at Nico, blushing a little. "A little much?"

"Something between this and what you probably grew up in." He nodded. "That's realistic."

"It's just a dream. I'd never be able to afford it."

"Never say never Bella. One day, you may have all your dreams come true."

I frowned at him. Nico slid out of the car, coming around to help me out, and then he grabbed the gifts from the trunk. With my hand in his, he led me up to the front steps. Before entering, he halted at the bottom.

"Bella, when the BBQ is over, there's something I need to talk to you about." There was a solemn look in his eyes.

He's serious. I nodded. "Okay."

Relief washed over his features. He kissed my cheek and proceeded to open the front door. The inside of the house is just as gorgeous as the outside. Welcoming and full without being gaudy with wealth. Women mulled around the kitchen, and they stared openly at me as Nico tugged me through. Pulling me out of a patio door, I gulped. There were so many people.

The backyard was massive. An outdoor kitchen stood just to the right of the doors. I could see a pool down a few steps on a lower tier. Tents and tables were set up for the event further out, and children could be seen playing on the grass and the blow-up contraptions further away. Nico tugged me to the group of men in the outdoor kitchen.

"Bella, meet my cousin Oliver Cantoni." Nico introduced. "Oliver, this is my girlfriend Roxanne Baxter."

I wasn't the only one stunned at being called Nico's girl-friend. We only went out on one date. I don't think we reached the point in our relationship where we can add labels to it. Though, it would be easier than saying 'the girl I'm dating' to everyone here. The man at the BBQ with light brown hair, short on the sides and long on top, recovered first. His green eyes sparkled with amusement as he extended a hand with a smile.

"A pleasure to meet you Roxanne."

"Likewise." I responded in kind, accepting the handshake.

Oliver tugged me forward, out of Nico's grasp. While keeping a tight grip on my hand, he spun me so my back hit his chest, and his arm then wrapped around my waist. He rested his chin on my shoulder and, with his free hand, shooed Nico.

"Why don't you put those gifts on the table by the bouncy castle." Oliver strongly suggested. "Then, on your way back, you can get Roxanne a drink."

"Oliver." Nico warned, his body tense.

"Your girlfriend is in excellent hands."

Nico looked to me for an answer. A laugh bubbled out of me. He'd have pulled me away from his cousin if he didn't trust his cousin. I smiled at Nico, relaxing into Oliver. *I'm not in any danger.* If I were uncomfortable, he'd pull me back into his arms.

"I'd love a lager." I told him.

Nico's shoulders slumped, but he nodded and left me in his cousin's hold. Once he was out of sight, Oliver let me go with a boisterous laugh. He introduced me to the other men hanging around the outdoor kitchen. They are all fathers to the kids they brought, who are friends of the birthday boy and girl. None related to Nico.

"You really are something special, Roxanne." Oliver stated, his smile never fading. "More than I pictured when he described you."

"I'm really not special." I assured him.

"I disagree." His smile faded as he took on a more serious note. "Nico shut himself off after what happened with Rachelle. I was honestly surprised when he came to me asking for reservations at Croquette. Now he's brought you here."

Rachelle? Who is that? Oliver dropped that name on purpose. I itched to know the story, but now is not the time to ask. And Oliver shouldn't be the one to tell me. If Nico and I ever discuss past relationships, then I can ask about Rachelle. For now, I'll let it drop. Instead, I latched onto what Oliver said about Croquette.

"Why would Nico go to you for reservations at Croquette?" I questioned.

"I own the restaurant."

My jaw fell open. Oliver laughed, echoed by the chuckles of the men around us. They obviously knew. A woman carrying two massive trays of meat entered the outdoor kitchen. Oliver immediately took the tray stacked with hamburger patties and put it down next to the tray of hot dogs she put down. He wrapped his arms around her, kissed her, then introduced her to me. Her wavy brown hair, cut in an angled bob, framed her face, highlighting her pink lips and cornflower blue eyes. *Her eyes are stunning.*

"I'm so glad I finally get to meet you Roxanne." Sonia smiled serenely. "Nico has told us a little about you."

"What has he said?" I questioned.

"Nothing bad, only positive." She waved away the question.

Just then, Nico appeared, handing me the requested lager. "Bella."

"Thank you." I took the bottle gratefully. "Your cousin owns Croquette."

Nico grinned. "Yes, yes, he does."

"Cheat." I grumbled.

146

He only chuckled. Wrapping an arm around my waist, he kissed my cheek. Sonia's smile widened. I wasn't in Nico's company long before she whisked me away to meet people. She was leading me to the pool on the lower tier of the backyard. She wrapped her arm around mine and gleefully introduced me to the women lounging in and by the water. I was careful where I stepped, keeping as much distance between myself and the edge of the pool as possible.

Eventually, Nico came to my rescue. He tucked me into his side and guided me to the lowest part of the backyard. Along the way, we were stopped by aunts, uncles and cousins, all wanting introductions. There were so many family members that I'll never remember all their names. We made it to the food table, he let go of me so we could fill our plates, and then we went to find a spot under a massive tent to eat.

"I'm sorry." Nico apologized.

"For what?"

"Today. It's a lot." He grimaced. "Maybe it was too soon to bring you to one of these events."

I took Nico's hand. "I'm a big girl. I can handle whatever question your family throws my way."

"Uncle Nico!"

A young boy and girl came rushing up to Nico. Whatever he was going to say to me vanished the moment he saw the children. He picked up the boy, seating him on his lap. The girl hid slightly behind Nico's chair. She looked up at me with big cornflower blue eyes.

"Toni, Annabelle, meet Roxanne." Nico introduced. "Roxanne, this is Toni and Annabelle. The birthday boy and girl."

They are spitting images of their parents. I smiled at them. "It's a pleasure to meet you both."

"Are you Uncle Nico's girlfriend?" Toni questioned me boldly.

"I am."

The boy eyed me. "I don't know if you're perfect enough for Uncle Nico."

"Toni." Nico bounced him lightly. "You're being rude."

"What would make me perfect for your uncle?" I questioned, playing along.

He pondered that question. "Do you love Uncle Nico?"

"Toni!" Nico scolded.

I laughed lightly. "I like Nico."

"But you don't love him." Toni persisted.

"Did you love your uncle right away?" I countered.

Toni pursed his lips. "I love him now."

"Love is not instant." I told him. "In time, I could come to love Nico, or we could realize we're not right for each other and break up."

"Uncle Nico deserves love."

"I completely agree."

The boy is precious. *Children really do say whatever is on their minds.* I looked up at Nico. He was watching me. I couldn't read his expression clearly. A tug on my hand drew my attention down. Annabelle had taken hold of my hand and was examining my nails.

"Do you like them?" I asked her.

She nodded.

"Would you like your nails done?"

Annabelle looked up at me, hope in her eyes. "Mama says I'm still too young."

"If you have nail polish, I can paint a unicorn on your nails."

The girl's face lit up with a smile. She tugged me out of the chair. I snagged a toothpick from my plate and struggled to catch my balance as she pulled me to the house and then upstairs. She opened the door to a purple and pink princess room. The room was the size of my whole apartment. Annabelle set me down at a small table and cleared the tea set. She then grabbed nail polish bottles and sat across from me.

Annabelle already wore a sparkly purple polish. Starting with white, I dipped the toothpick into the polish on the brush, then proceeded to draw the head of a unicorn on each of her thumbnails. Black for the eye. Pink for the mane. Silver for the horn.

"There you are." Sonia appeared in the doorway. "Your brother wants to start opening presents."

"Mama, look what Aunty Roxy did." Annabelle ran to her mom.

"Pretty. Now, what do you say?"

Annabelle came running back to me and threw her arms around me. "Thank you Aunty Roxy."

"You're welcome and happy birthday."

Annabelle ran out of the room. I closed up the bottles and stood. Sonia waited for me by the door.

"Annabelle is a shy girl. I have never seen her warm up to anyone as quickly as she did you."

"That's the power of unicorns." I grinned.

Sonia laughed. "You're going to have to come over every weekend now, Aunty Roxy."

I laughed. "All part of my master plan."

Sonia stopped me at the bottom of the stairs. "Nico's been hurt badly once."

"Rachelle?"

She nodded. "Oliver told you that name, didn't he?"

"I really do like Nico." I told her honestly.

"Oliver and I are the only family Nico trusts. He's told us about your date at Croquette and your brother." Sonia said. "You don't have to hide or be careful around us."

"Thank you." It felt like a weight was taken off my shoulders.

"I'll give you my number if you ever want to talk."

"You'll have to write it down for me." I gave her an awkward smile. "I took my SIM card out so my brother can't track me."

Sonia blinked, then laughed. "I like you more and more, Roxanne."

Sixteen

NICO

I WATCHED ANNABELLE DRAG Roxanne away. My heart swelled at the sight. *She's so good with kids.* Toni nagged me about the gift I got him, drawing my attention back to my nephew, and I reminded him that his gift was a surprise. He'll have to wait. His friends came running up to drag him back to the play area.

I went to find Oliver. The toys should have been delivered, and I'd need his help to move the gifts from the front door to the living room. After moving the gifts, I was pulled into conversations with aunts and uncles who questioned me about Roxanne and proclaimed that she was not good enough for me. The single women attending the party also flocked around me. Despite seeing me with Roxanne earlier, they flirted like she was just a fling, and they had an actual chance with me.

I looked toward the house. *When will Roxanne return?* I didn't realize how much of a shield she was until this very moment. A screech drew everyone's attention to the bar. I sighed, recognizing that all-too-familiar sound. Excusing myself from the women around me, I went to find my sister. I found her in a catfight with Irene, their hands tangled in each other's hair and a crowd forming around them.

"Break it up." I hollered, breaking through to wrap my arms around Candi's waist. "Let her go Candi."

My sister refused to listen. I've never understood why these two could never get along. I looked around for Brina but couldn't find her. I tugged Candi back. She hissed at me and strained to scratch Irene's eyes out. This is the first time these two have gotten into a physical fight. Usually, they are found in a verbal spar.

Irene is my uncle's mistress. He met her three years ago and claimed she made him feel young again. Every time I saw them together, though, they never appeared to be romantically involved. Instead, the blonde consistently flirted with me. Her flirting didn't feel genuine either. It felt forced. I told my uncle about her advances, but he didn't seem to care that his mistress was looking for entertainment elsewhere.

"What is going on?" Sonia demanded, rushing up to the scene. "Irene! Candi! Break it up!"

Still, the women clawed at each other. Someone had finally wrapped their arms around Irene. With quite a lot of effort, we pulled the women apart. Candi and Irene's feet kicked out, and their arms extended. Even from a distance, they were still trying to attack the other. *What has gotten into them?* I've never seen Candi get physically violent before.

"Cristo, Candi, fermare." I growled.

"I've had it with her." Candi growled back.

"Princess, if you break a nail, I'm not fixing it." Roxanne stated firmly.

Candi stiffened in my arms and looked down at her hands. "No, you can't."

"How dare you fight in front of my children." Sonia tsked. "On their birthday, no less."

"She threw her drink at me." Candi defended and pointed a finger at Irene.

"It was an accident." Irene countered. "Even if it weren't, you would have deserved it."

"You ruined my outfit."

"Don't." Sonia warned, putting up a hand to silence them both. "I want both of you out of my house. You've overstayed your welcome today."

They fell silent, glaring at each other. Sonia gave a warning look to both Irene and Candi before heading off to the present table where Toni had been waiting impatiently for his sister. Roxanne stepped in front of Candi and took hold of her hands. I kept an eye on Irene to make sure she didn't do something stupid with Sonia's back turned. I swear I saw recognition flash across her face when she saw Roxanne. It was so quick, though. I could have been mistaken.

"You're lucky." Roxanne told Candi. "No damage done."

"You can let me go now Nico." Candi requested.

I let my sister go and tucked Roxanne into my side. "A testament to Bella's work."

Brina came rushing over with two bags on her shoulders. "We should go Candi. That stain is only going to be harder to get out the longer it goes untreated."

"Yes." Candi acknowledged. "Let's go. The party has soured anyway."

Taking a bag from Brina, the two of them left. I shook my head. Fashion and nails are the only two things that seem to concern my sister. My gut told me there was more to her fight with Irene than simply a spilled drink, but now wasn't the time to look into it. Despite Sonia's order to leave, I knew Irene was going to stay until my uncle wanted to leave.

"Let's go watch the presents get unwrapped."

"You head over there." Roxanne stated. "I'm just going to grab a drink first."

"I'll come with you." I offered.

"I'm a big girl. I can get my own drink."

Roxanne slipped out of my hold and approached the full-service bar. For family events, Oliver and Sonia hire a bartender. On an average day, there's only wine, beer, water, and pop for guests to serve themselves. Just as I turned to head to the present table, I saw Irene saddle up to the bar next to Roxanne. I mentally prayed that Irene and Roxanne wouldn't get into a fight next. I glanced over my shoulder, but their backs were to me. I couldn't see if they were talking to each other, but they both appeared relaxed. *Maybe they know each other, but how would they know each other?*

Roxanne joined me shortly after at the present table with a beer in hand. Toni and Annabelle were already halfway through their gift opening. I could see the gifts Roxanne had brought were still unopened. One by one, the wrapping on boxes was ripped, and tissue paper flew out of gift bags. When Roxanne's gifts were opened, I squeezed her side appreciatively. Toni received a remote-controlled car, and Annabelle received nail polish. The gifts were simple and mundane, yet perfect for my niece and nephew.

I kissed her cheek. "Excellent choices."

"I can't tell if they like it." Roxanne admitted. "They've been going from gift to gift without much thought."

"There's a lot to open."

"Your family is opulent in their gifts."

I chuckled. "None of that compares to what I got them."

When all the gifts were unwrapped, Toni looked up at his dad. "Where's Uncle Nico's gift?"

"It's in the living room." Oliver stated.

"I want to open it."

"First, say thank you to your family and friends."

Toni beamed at the crowd that had formed. "Thank you."

Annabelle shyly thanked everyone as well. Toni ran off toward the house with Oliver, and the crowd dispersed from the area. Now that the main event is done, they'll slowly start heading home. Annabelle came up to Roxanne, taking her hand. Roxanne knelt to be at eye level with her.

"Aunty Roxy, what present did you get me?" Annabelle asked.

"Let me show you."

Roxanne stood, moved to the table and pointed out her gift. I watched my niece's face brighten with a smile. She tugged Roxanne back down and kissed her cheek. I could hear the gasps around me. *That does it. My heart is lost.* My woman just won over the shyest little girl I've ever seen. My gut tightened. I still have to tell Roxanne about my father. She may walk out of my life forever after she hears what I have to say to her. If that happens, Annabelle is going to be disappointed. Who am I kidding, I may not recover if I lose Roxanne.

"Thank you Uncle Nico!" Toni slammed into my leg for a hug. "I love the car."

"I'm glad." I patted his head.

The party lasted about an hour longer before it began to dwindle. The kids and their parents were the first to leave, yawning as their parents picked them up to head home. Toni and Annabelle were tucked away in bed, insisting that Roxanne and I did it. Oliver set up a poker table and was scolded by Sonia for not helping clean up, then, with a sheepish grin, started helping. In no time, the leftover food was put away, the glasses were cleaned up around the yard, and the garbage was collected. The air was taken out of the bouncy castle, the food tent, tables, and chairs were left out to be dealt with in the morning, and the presents were brought in.

"Okay." Oliver clapped his hands, rubbing them together. "Who wants to play?"

A nephew, his girlfriend, an uncle, and another cousin all pulled up chairs. Very few guests remained. The few that did remain didn't have children, and the atmosphere shifted to a much more relaxed evening.

"Bella?" I turned to her.

"You play." She said. "I'm going to the washroom. When I get back, I'll be your good luck charm."

I kissed her cheek, then pulled up a chair to the poker table. Oliver dealt me in. We were a couple of rounds in when I glanced at the house. *Where is she?* Roxanne should have been back by now. I folded and excused myself.

I started down the hall to the bathroom and froze. The sight before me made my blood boil. Franco held Roxanne's wrists at her side, pressing her into the wall, and he was kissing her. I saw red. Itching to rip my brother off her and punch him, my hands balled into fists at my side.

I took a step forward and stopped. Roxanne kneed Franco. I couldn't help but grin at his growl of pain. He'd taken a half step back, hunching forward slightly. Roxanne shoved at his chest, forcing him back further. Franco still wouldn't let go of her wrists. Roxanne stepped to the side, took hold of his wrists, and yanked him forward. She kept one foot in his path so he'd trip on it. The momentum sent him face-first into the wall.

Franco let go of Roxanne in favour of holding his nose. As turned on as I am by her, a sliver of fear snaked up my spine. *What will Franco do now?* There's no way he'll let Roxanne get away with attacking him, even if it was well deserved. Roxanne backed quickly away from my brother.

"Impressive." I praised.

Roxanne looked embarrassed when she turned to see me. "Nico."

I pulled her into me and glared at my brother. "Touch her again, in any way, and I'll make sure you regret it."

Franco laughed. His eyes glittered with amusement. "You can't protect that Farfalla forever."

My grip on Roxanne tightened. "You have no respect."

"Let's go home." Roxanne pleaded softly.

I couldn't agree more. We said our goodbyes to the remaining guests before heading out. Roxanne stayed tucked in my side, but the moment I helped her into the car, it felt like she put up a wall. Roxanne sat angled away from me and stared out the window. I don't know if Franco said anything, but if he did, then it couldn't have been good.

"Not my place."

Roxanne spoke up when she realized the direction I was heading. I glanced at her, but she didn't look my way. I took her instead to my place. She didn't say anything when I parked or on the ride up the elevator. She didn't even say anything when she entered my penthouse.

Roxanne removed her shoes in the entryway by the door. Placing her purse on the breakfast bar, she looked around.

I watched her. Her expression didn't change. *I wish I knew what was going through her head.* Roxanne wandered over to the floor-to-ceiling window in the living room. The view that overlooks Frostham is beautiful. Tonight, I couldn't see the city lights. All I could see was Roxanne. She placed a hand on the glass and looked out. The penthouse was dark, the only light coming from the moon. The moon's light shone through the window, giving her a halo effect.

Entranced, I went to her, wrapping my arms around her waist and resting my chin on her shoulder. She leaned back into me, her hands on my forearms. I will never tire of holding Roxanne in my arms. We locked eyes in the reflection of the glass. For the longest time, we just stood there.

"Today was nice." She said softly. "I like your family."

"My whole family or just my cousin?"

Her lips tilted upward. "Sonia and Oliver. They really care for you."

"They seem to like you a lot too."

"Before the BBQ, you said you had something to tell me afterward."

I tightened my hold on her. "I did. Did Franco say anything to you before he rudely placed his lips on you?"

"He said you have a secret and that you can't be trusted."

"Bastardo." I grumbled.

Roxanne watched me. "He also said that within a month, I will be his."

"That is never going to happen." I told her firmly.

"Nico, what did you want to talk to me about?" Her nails dug into my forearms. "Does it have anything to do with what Franco said?"

"Bella." I tried not to wince at my pleading tone. "I don't know what Franco said, but."

Her lips thinned, but she didn't pull away from me. I needed her in my arms for this confession. It might be the last time I'll ever get to hold her.

"That day, in your office, when I asked you out, I knew who you were. I knew your brother and father were cops. I knew they wanted to put me and the rest of my family in jail. I didn't care. I'd decided that asking you out would be worth the risk." I maintained eye contact through the glass reflection and kept this honest. "I thought seducing you would be beneficial to getting me out of my father's shadow. Prove to him and the family that I don't want to be connected to the Frangione business. I wanted to have you as my witness that I have nothing to do with them if your brother or father ever slapped the cuffs on me."

Roxanne took in a sharp breath.

"That kiss distracted me." I continued. "Our date turned my plan on its side. One evening with you, and I only wanted you. I wanted to see you again. I needed to be with you."

My grip on her tightened, my forehead falling to her shoulder. I couldn't look her in the eye. Afraid to see the hurt and the hatred I know I've caused. *I should let her go.* I know I should, but it's difficult. I felt Roxanne's hands drop, so slowly, reluctantly, I let my arms fall. Roxanne, though, didn't move away. We just stood there, my head on her shoulder, our only point of contact.

"Seeing Franco kiss you reminded me how much danger you're in just by knowing me."

"I took a chance on you." She said, her voice a little raw, as if she was holding back tears. "I told you my brother is a cop because I didn't want you to think I was using you. My brother warned me that you are dangerous, but I ignored him and listened to my friends because of how you make me feel."

I dared to look up. Roxanne sported an emotionless mask. Her eyes shone with the unshed tears that I could hear in her voice. She was holding back. I itched to wrap her back in my arms.

"I took a chance, knowing that I could wind up getting hurt if my father puts you in jail." She continued. "But this, Nico, knowing that you knew more about me from day one than I let you know, hurts."

"Bella. Non era mia intenzione ferirti." I admitted, then translated. "It wasn't my intention to hurt you."

"Why me?" She demanded. "Forget about my family. Why would you ask me out on a date?"

I stared at her, uncertain how to answer. She challenged me like no other woman. After that first kiss in her office, I became addicted, needing her like I needed my next breath. The only way I can think to convey how I feel is to throw her over my shoulder and take her to bed, but she wants words, not actions. Roxanne wrapped her arms around herself, the tears finally falling. I took too long to answer.

"Tell me, Nico. Or this is the last time you'll ever see me again."

I can't lose her, but I couldn't bring the words I wanted to convey forward. She stepped away, ducking her head as she began to leave. Panicked, I turned to catch her. Turning, my foot caught on the coffee table leg, and my knees fell onto the couch. Reaching over the back of the couch, I took hold of her arm. She didn't stop. My grip slid down to her wrist.

"Ti sei il mio sole, Bella." I blurted out.

Roxanne froze. Two arm's length away, I needed her closer. I gripped her wrist tighter. I only have right now. If she leaves then she's lost forever.

"You are my sunshine, Bella." I repeated.

Roxanne stood there, unmoving. She was waiting for me. She was waiting to see if I had more to say before she walked out of my penthouse. Honesty is my only weapon to keep her.

"Before I met you, I was stuck in my father's shadow, unable to break free. I tried to get away by starting my own business, but his shadow still loomed over me, threatening to draw me back into the darkness. Then I met you. You make me feel like I can finally step out from my father's shadow and stand proudly in the light." I took a deep breath and continued to bear my soul to this woman. "You see me as me, Bella. You see Nico Frangione, the man, not Nico Frangione, son to Enzo."

"Enzo?" Roxanne stiffened. Slowly, she turned to me, her eyes wide. "Enzo, is your father?"

"Yes." I answered hesitantly.

"He killed my grandpa — in front of my dad."

"Cristo."

I let my hand drop. Roxanne will walk out the door and never look back now. I can't blame her. Both my father and my brother have screwed up my life — again. First with Rachelle, now with Roxanne. I let my head drop, my hands gripping the back of the couch. Despair, anger, and darkness are all I'm allowed to have in my life, apparently. Happiness will never be my future.

"You should go." I mumbled, defeated. "Before I hurt you even more, Bella."

To my surprise, Roxanne gently took my face in her hands. Her hazel eyes still glistened with tears as she stared at me, but there was something else in them. Something I couldn't read, or maybe that I didn't understand. *Is this her final goodbye?*

"You have a lot to apologize for." She kissed me softly. "It'll take a lot for me to forgive you, but I am willing to let you try and get back into my good graces."

"Bella." I breathed out, relief and hope filling my heart.

I kissed her, my arms wrapping around her waist and pulling her close. The couch, though, is in my way. Without breaking contact with Roxanne, I climbed over the back. Foot getting caught, I hopped in place until I could get both feet on the floor. Roxanne stopped kissing me to giggle. Fucking giggled. It was the sweetest sound I've ever heard. I wanted to bottle it up and preserve it.

I smiled at her. "I've got to hear that again."

"Hear what?"

"That giggle."

I gripped her ass and lifted her effortlessly in my arms. The suddenness of the action elicited a squeal from her. She quickly wrapped her arms and legs around me.

"I wonder what other sounds you can make."

A mischievous smile graced her lips. "Care to find out?"

"Cazzo sì." I growled.

I carried her to my room. Placing her feet on the floor, she stepped back to undress. I stared at her naked body hungrily.

"Bellissima."

Roxanne blushed. "You're not playing fair."

"How so?"

"I'm naked, and you're not."

"Easily fixed."

I quickly undressed before my lips found hers again. I walked her back to the bed. We fell down together, our lips never parting, and she shimmied further on the mattress.

"I'm going to worship every inch of your body, as promised." I told her, my hands skimming down her sides. "By the end of the night, your throat is going to be raw from screaming my name. We are going to break records."

"Nico." Roxanne moaned.

"I'm going to fuck you hard into this mattress Bella."

"Yes, Nico." She arched into my touch. "Speak Italian to me."

"Sei la donna più bella che abbia mai posato gli occhi."

"Oh, Nico."

"You are the most beautiful woman I've ever laid eyes on." I slid two fingers into her folds and groaned. "Cristo, Bella, you're so wet, and I've only just gotten started."

With my hands and mouth, I teased her, tasted her, and brought her to orgasm.

"Oh god. Nico." She exclaimed.

"That's it Bella." I urged. "Sing for me. We have all night."

I reached for a condom in the side table drawer. I ached to be inside her. I've been wanting this since that first kiss in her office. I will extend her pleasure and mine. Tonight will be the first of many nights.

Seventeen

ROXANNE

I snuggled deeper into the warmth of the bed sheets, my body completely sated and sore in all the right places. I smiled to myself as the memory of Nico hovering over me, our bodies entwined, clawed through my morning haze. Reaching out, I felt for him but found the bed empty. Opening my eyes, I frowned at the empty space.

He's not here. Cold washed over me. His confession last night, the one about how he feels about me, was like a balm over the hurt of his admission of wanting to use me. It was that confession mixed with all the lust that's been building between us that led me to his bed. Maybe I moved too fast. Perhaps the confession was a ploy, and he's still using me. *No.* I shook my head. *There was honesty reflected in his gaze.*

A door opened, and Nico stepped out. He stood there in a pair of grey sweatpants and a satisfied smile. Steam billowed around him. The sight of Nico eased the worry tightening in my chest. When he came closer, I noticed his hair was still damp. Nico bent down to kiss me.

"Have a shower." He instructed. "I'll make breakfast. You can slip into one of my shirts."

"Okay." I mumbled.

Nico chuckled and, after another peck on my lips, left the bedroom. I heard him moving around in the kitchen and decided I couldn't stay in bed forever. I flung the sheets off and strode quickly to the lovely, warm bathroom. The tile floor felt warm beneath my feet. I sighed at the luxury. I've always wanted subfloor heating for my bathroom, but it's a luxury I can't afford. I survive with a simple store-bought portable heater for the winter. I took in the bathroom. Nico has a large soaker tub, easily big enough for two people, and a massive glass-enclosed shower. As much as I'd love to take a bath in that tub, the shower is all I have time for.

I turned on the water and lifted my head. The hot liquid rained down on me — literally — Nico's shower head is a wide square above my head. The water rained down with the perfect amount of pressure. I relaxed in the soothing rhythm. I used Nico's shampoo and body wash. Fresh air scented, clean and subtle. Once washed, I stepped out and dried off with the fluffiest of towels.

I don't have a toothbrush, and I'm not about to search the cupboards for one. Squeezing some toothpaste on my finger, I ran it along my teeth. It'll have to be good enough to get rid of any morning breath until I get home. Leaving the bathroom, I entered Nico's walk-in closet and pulled down a dress shirt. It hit me mid-thigh, and the sleeves dangled a few inches past my fingers.

Before stepping out of the bedroom, I took a deep breath. The bedroom felt safe, while beyond the door, I'd be exposed. No longer wrapped up in intimacy, I have no idea how to act around Nico. The man looked up from what he was doing when I opened the door. It wasn't until I was closer that I could see the lust and appreciation in his dilated eyes. It banished any previous concerns I may have had. I sat at the breakfast bar and pulled my purse over.

"What are you making?" I questioned while pulling out my phone.

"Pancakes."

"Smells delicious."

He smiled shyly. "I hope it tastes delicious."

I frowned at him. "Why wouldn't it be?"

"I've never made pancakes before."

"Then why make them?"

He flipped the pancakes over to cook the other side. "To impress you."

I couldn't help but smile. "I'm impressed you're making an effort."

I put the SIM card back into my phone. The device buzzed continuously as all the text messages and missed call notifications came flooding in. I frowned. It was a mix of messages from both Jaylen and Tyler. Their messages started simple, and they grew to sound more desperate as the day went on when I wasn't answering.

The phone rang while in my hands. Cringing, I answered and placed it to my ear. "Ty."

"Rox." My brother heaved a huge sigh.

"What's wrong?"

"Where are you?" His tone turned serious, with a warning undertone. "Are you okay? You turned your phone off yesterday."

"I'm fine. I turned it off to not be disturbed."

"You weren't at home, at mom and dad's, or even at work. Lexi said you were on a date. Was it with Nico Frangione?"

"You told me to stay away from Nico." I answered evasively.

"So? You never listen to me."

"That's not true. I believe you when you say he's dangerous, so I'm being careful."

He paused. "What did he do?"

"Nothing you, Jaylen, dad, or any other police officer needs to worry about."

"Roxanne." He growled in annoyance.

"I have to go, Tyler. Breakfast just arrived. I love you."

I hung up and double-checked that the location was still off. I certainly don't want him to know where I am and try to 'rescue' me. Nico removed the pancakes from the griddle, placing them on a plate. He looked at me with a single raised brow.

"I'm dangerous?"

"Yes." I nodded. "Dangerously charming and sexy."

His lips curled into a smirk. "You seem to have a resistance to my charm, Bella."

"Nope." I smiled, following him to the table he'd set up. "Your charm had me falling into bed with you."

"Then I hope I can charm you back into it again tonight."

"Not even Italian can do that."

"Sei sicuro?"

I shivered, a small smile on my lips. "I don't know what that means, but I can't come over tonight. Every Sunday, it's supper with the family."

"Tomorrow?" He asked, hopeful.

"We'll see. Can you do lunch on Tuesday?" I hesitated while I poured maple syrup, the real stuff, over three pancakes. "I'd like you to meet my mom."

Nico froze. "Your mom?"

"Yes, my mom." I glanced up through my lashes. "It'll mean a lot if you can gain her approval."

"What about your dad?"

"He's going to be a challenge." I bit my lip. "The Frangione name is a black spot in his book."

Nico nodded solemnly. "Can you tell me the story? About the day your grandfather passed?"

"Mmm." I moaned as I took my first bite of pancake. "These are delicious. Did you add cinnamon?"

"I did." He said, letting me avoid his question.

"I love it."

He smiled proudly at his first pancake attempt. We fell silent as we ate. It wasn't uncomfortable, but there was a hint of tension between us. I know I should tell him the story. It'll help us move forward, but I'm not sure how to begin. I was only a kid when it happened. When I was older and demanded to know what happened to Grandpa, Dad finally told me. Though, I swear it was still censored. The events of that day changed dad, even if he tried not to show it around Tyler and me.

I helped Nico clean up, insisting on washing the dishes since he cooked. Nico gave in and dried, then put the dishes away. Once finished, I turned to him. My eyes caught on the tattoo on his chest. I remember seeing it in the photo he sent, but I didn't get a good look at it, and I definitely didn't pay much attention last night. I reached out and lightly ran my fingertips around the outside of the design. A dragon curled around an egg that lay on a pile of coins. The black line work was striking.

"It's beautiful."

Nico took my hand, kissing the palm. "It's symbolic."

I looked up at him. "For what?"

"I protect what's mine." He placed my hand on his chest and kissed me. "And you're mine, Bella."

I blushed. I need to tell him before we move any further. Taking a step back, I moved around the breakfast bar and took a seat. I twisted my fingers together, staring at them. I could feel Nico's eyes on me.

"Dad was about to be promoted from uniform to plain clothes homicide detective." I started. "Grandpa, proud of his son, went on his last car ride in uniform with him. It was a pretty mundane day. That is until the call came in. All available units were to head to a warehouse district where a shootout was happening. When Dad and Grandpa arrived, there were already so many police officers open firing at people just inside the warehouse. According to Dad, Grandpa claimed they should go around back and catch the shooters off guard. As they came around, two men were leaving."

Closing my eyes, I took a deep breath. I could still see the smiling face of the man who would put me on his shoulders during a Christmas parade. The kind man who would spoil me because I was his favourite granddaughter, his only granddaughter, but it didn't matter. His death was devastating.

"Dad said that grandpa called out to the older of the two men, Antonio Frangione. The older man ordered Enzo to get in the car. Enzo opened the car door, and with a nasty smile, he pulled out a gun and shot grandpa so fast that neither of them could react. Enzo and Antonio drove off. Dad fired at the car but couldn't go after them. Because of the shootout happening in the front of the building, the ambulance didn't make it in time."

"Bella." Nico rested his hands over mine. "I'm sorry."

"I know there's more to the story, but that's all Dad would ever tell me."

"Antonio is an uncle. He took over the family business when my grandfather passed. My father took over once he had a firm grasp of the business's inner workings." Nico told me. "I was young, but I remember Antonio cursing when he returned home one day. He went on a tirade, claiming someone within the ranks snitched to the cops about the deal."

172

"What deal?"

"No idea. The last thing I heard before father and Antonio sealed themselves off in the office was Antonio telling him he shouldn't have shot Carlos. My father was in charge for only a week at this point."

"Carlos, that was my grandpa's name." Emotion caught in my throat.

"I didn't know."

"Now you do." I pulled my hands back, taking a minute to collect myself. "Dad will never stop coming after you or your family. It's personal."

Nico came around the breakfast bar and cupped my face. "Bella, this dark history of ours should not mould our future. If your father tries to hide you away from me, I will find you. If my father tries to harm you, I will be your shield."

"Really?" I looked at him cautiously hopeful.

"Bella." Nico chuckled. "After that first kiss in your office, I knew there would be nothing that'll keep me from you. You're mine."

My heart swelled. Nico is nothing like the stories and rumours I've heard over the years about his father. Yes, there is a darkness to him that'll make him dangerous. Especially when angry. I've seen flashes of it, but he's never turned that darkness on me. He's been nothing but kind. I can't hold back, not if I want to try to have a relationship with Nico.

"I'm yours." I told him confidently.

Nico kissed me firmly, possessively. I melted into him. My phone chose that moment to ring. Pulling back, I answered it.

Nico wasn't deterred. His lips trailed down my neck, and his fingers began undoing the buttons of his shirt that I'd slipped on.

"Hello?"

"Rox, you need to get to the salon." Lexi urged. "Like yesterday."

I sat up a little straighter, placing a hand on Nico's chest. "What's going on Lexi?"

"There's a warrant for cameras."

Hell no. What is my brother thinking? Unless this is Dad's idea. Fear twisted my gut.

"I'm getting dressed." I told her and hung up.

"What's going on?" Nico inquired, stepping back.

I slid off the chair. "Can you drive me to the salon?"

"Of course."

We both got dressed. I asked Nico to drop me off a block away, not wanting anyone to see him with me. When I came running down the block, I saw two police cars in front of the salon. Fresh clothes would make this easier, but that's another problem. Cameras are more pressing. Stepping inside, Lexi looked relieved to see me. She handed me the warrant. I read it carefully. Fury took over. Leaving my purse on the counter with Lexi, I stormed off in search of my brother. I found him out back with Jaylen. They were watching an officer put a camera above the back door.

"This is going too far." I snarled, slamming the warrant into Tyler's chest. "Take them all down."

"No."

"Rox, it's for your safety." Jaylen countered.

"No. This is personal. Nico has nothing to do with grandpa's death."

Tyler's face twisted into one of fury. "Frangione is responsible for murder, drugs, and kidnapping. And he's been seen here multiple times."

"You have no proof it's Nico, or else you'd have had him behind bars already." I stood toe to toe with my brother. "What about his older brother? Are you putting just as much effort into looking into him as you are, Nico? Or are you hell-bent on pinning every crime on Nico, whether he's innocent or guilty?"

"I'm not discussing the case with you, Roxanne."

"Placing cameras in my place of business will not help your case detective." I emphasized his title with as much disgust as I could muster at this moment.

"There is nothing you can do about the warrant. A judge approved these cameras." Ty glared. "Live with it sis."

I slapped him. There was a moment of stunned silence between all of us. No one moved, no one spoke. The officer attaching the camera dropped something. Its clatter seemed to break the spell.

"Roxanne." Jaylen wrapped his arms around me to hold my arms at my side. "You're overreacting."

I slammed my foot on the inside of Jaylen's foot. He cursed, letting go of me. Tyler took hold of me and handcuffed my wrists behind my back. I struggled. My shoulder came up to hit my brother in the jaw. He stumbled back, and Jaylen took over. He hobbled me over to his car, shoved me into the back and sealed me within. Laying on my back, I pounded at the window with my feet.

Jaylen and Tyler returned to work. It was pointless. They weren't going to let me out anytime soon. I sat there fuming. Sure, slapping my brother was a little excessive, but so was putting cameras in my salon. Dad's name was nowhere on the warrant, which means he knows nothing about this. I could squeal on him, but it won't do me any good. As soon as Nico's name is brought up, Dad will side with Tyler and yell at us both for not telling him about this sooner. Mom might take my side and help me upturn the warrant, but she doesn't know I'm seeing Nico — not until she meets him on Tuesday for lunch.

Eventually, Jaylen returned to his car. Instead of letting me out, he drove me home. The infuriating man walked me up to my apartment before setting me free of the handcuffs. I took my purse from him and let myself in.

"I'm sorry about this, Rox." He said. "But it really is for your safety."

"How is it for my safety?" I countered.

"Nico is dangerous, and as Tyler said, we know he's been around Dagger Designs. We don't want you getting caught up in the case."

I gripped the door handle to stop myself from slapping him, too. "If you and Ty had talked to me first, we could have discussed this."

With a glare, I slammed the door in his face and locked it. I checked my phone. Nico's number and texts are still there, but

I don't trust that my brother didn't make a clone. I changed into fresh clothes and went back out. *I'll get a second phone.*

Eighteen

NICO

AFTER DROPPING ROXANNE off at her salon, I returned to my condo building and went straight to the security office on the main floor. A beefy man with sharp brown eyes nodded at my approach. His short salt-and-pepper hair and erect posture when standing hinted at his previous profession of being ex-military. Paul eased into retirement as the condo building's security. Because of Paul, this is the safest building to live in Frostham. Not that the city is unsafe. Records show that there hasn't been a burglary attempt or vandalism since Paul's been hired.

"Hey Paul."

"Mr. Frangione. What can I do for you?"

I leaned my forearms on the elevated part of his desk. "How would I go about adding someone to my approved visitor list?"

Paul's lips quirked, but he didn't grin. "It's not that hard. All I need is their name. When they arrive at the front door, they can call the general line and pass along their name to be let in."

"What if I want to give this person a code to enter the building and a key to my penthouse?"

"I can do that from here." He turned to the computer. "Who is this person?"

"Roxanne Baxter."

I could see the smile form on Paul's face as he typed. I could only imagine what was going through his head.

"Does she have a car?"

"Yes."

"Make, model, and licence plate?"

I pulled out my phone to read off all that information from a text my hacker friend sent me. Knowing I was coming down here to add Roxanne to the approved list of visitors, I made sure I had all of her information. I want her over as often as possible. Having her own code and key will just be more straightforward. She won't have to wait for me.

"That's done." Paul stated a smile now permanently on his face. "I was hoping you didn't have this information."

"Why?" I put my phone away.

"I wanted to meet Miss Baxter."

I grinned. I'm sure he's seen her on the security cameras, but that pales in comparison to the real thing. Paul stood from his seat and entered another room behind him. I could hear a machine start-up, and in a few short minutes, he returned. Paul wrote something down before handing me a sticky note and a plain brass key.

"Miss Baxter's access code and key to your penthouse. Let me know if you need her access revoked. I'll have the lock to your penthouse changed as well."

"Thanks Paul."

"No problem Mr. Frangione. I hope you bring Miss Baxter around sometime." Paul winked. "For security reasons, I like to meet all the visitors on the approved list."

I pocketed the key and code and headed to the elevators. I couldn't wipe the grin from my face all the way up. Roxanne is the first woman I've brought back to my place. She's also the first woman I've wanted since Rachelle. I imagined Roxanne's slow smile when I hand her the key and how she could thank me for the honour. Now that we've both exposed some secrets that we've been withholding since the first meeting, I feel like we can genuinely have a real relationship with her. The second I stepped foot into my place, my phone rang. Looking at the caller ID, I frowned, not recognizing the number. I answered cautiously.

"Hello?"

"Nico, It's Roxanne."

I looked at the caller ID again. "You got a new number."

"I did."

"May I ask why?"

"My brother and I had an altercation." She sighed heavily. "Call it paranoia. I'm not sure if he decided to clone my phone, so I got a second one, just in case."

"Bella." My gut tightened. "If seeing me is going to affect your relationship with your family."

"Don't." She cut me off firmly. "This is my choice Nico. I want to have a relationship with you. The altercation was partly my fault, mostly Tyler's, but I overreacted and didn't think things through."

I chuckled. "It seems all older brothers are getting on your bad side as of late."

She laughed. "Seems that way."

"Do you want to talk about it?"

Roxanne let out a defeated little sound. "He got a warrant to put cameras in my salon."

Furry washed over me. I had to take a moment before speaking. "He has no right. If I ever cross paths with him, I'll punch him for you."

"Thank you." She snickered.

"I know you said you have a family dinner tonight, but are you sure you still want to go?"

"I will." She said, determined. "And Nico?"

"Yes Bella?"

"Don't punch my brother. It'll only give him a reason to arrest you."

My heart soared. *She's worried for me.* After everything, she's still my ray of sunshine in this darkness.

"I promise not to punch your brother the first time I meet him." I promised.

Roxanne was silent a beat. "Or the second time. In fact, punching my brother is off limits."

I chuckled. "You're ruining my fun."

"I'm saving your ass. Dragons don't do well in captivity." I could hear the smile in her voice before she said goodbye and hung up.

Roxanne hung up just in time because I heard the elevator ping on the other side of my front door. Then came the knock. With a frown, I opened the door only to be met with my father. Standing tall and opposing, he wore a semi-permanent scowl.

"Father."

"Nico, my boy." He sounded almost pleased. "Are you not going to let me in?"

I stepped to the side. He strode in like he owned the place. Maybe he does. I made a mental note to look into that. If he does, it would explain how he got into the building. After closing the door, I watched him. My father looked around, assessing my living arrangements. With an approving nod, he turned to me.

"Are you not going to offer me a drink?"

I shook my head. "Why are you here, father?"

"So rude." He scoffed while perching on the edge of the breakfast bar stool. "Can I not stop by to see my son?"

"That's not like you." Despite myself, I still fetched him a glass of whiskey.

"I was hoping you were with the Baxter girl. I wanted to meet her."

My shoulders stiffened. "She has a business to run."

"Right." He nodded, accepting the drink. "That nail place."

"Why are you here, father?"

"Since she's not here, you can provide me with an update."

"Franco nearly screwed things up." I sneered.

My father's dark eyes turned colder. "Don't talk badly about your brother."

"Right, your perfect son can't do anything wrong."

"Nico." He warned darkly.

"Franco made a move that nearly had her running back to her family."

"Nearly?"

"I salvaged his mess."

"Lavoro eccelente." The smallest of smiles ghosted past his lips, hidden by the whiskey glass he sipped from. "Now that you've created a stronger bond with the girl, gathering intel shouldn't be too hard."

My mind whirled. "Did you and Franco plan that?"

"I'm leaving the city for business." He declared. "I shouldn't be gone long."

"Father?"

He stood, tugging the cuffs of his suit. "When I return, I expect positive news."

With that, he left. If that whole Franco meets Roxanne scene had been planned, then I should have let her go that night. If I did let her go, then who knows what Franco would do next.

"Fottermi!"

Roxanne is mine in every sense of the word. I won't let Franco touch her. Somehow, I need to get the information my father wants without breaking Roxanne's tentative trust in me.

I texted my hacker friend to see if he could hack into the police system. The answer, unfortunately, is yes, but only for a short time. I'd need to know precisely what he should be looking for not to get caught hacking. It'll be easier if he is directly connected, but that's a risk neither of us is willing to take. Not wanting my friend to get arrested for helping me hack the police, I told him not to do anything right now.

Nineteen

ROXANNE

I WALKED INTO THE dealership, nervous about taking Nico to meet my mom. She doesn't know I'm bringing Nico. I need someone other than my friends to confirm my gut feeling that Nico isn't as bad as Dad and Tyler keep making him out to be. It has to be someone who won't be easily charmed by him. Mom is that someone. She used to be a prosecutor, helping the police put criminals in jail. She's tough but has always had a good sense of people. I need her judgment. I'm not sure what I'll do if she disapproves of Nico.

"Miss Bella Baxter."

I stopped, startled out of my thoughts, and turned to the voice. The receptionist was standing, looking like she was going to leave her post to grab my attention. *I have got to get out of my head.*

"Yes?" I answered cautiously.

The dark-skinned beauty offered me an easy smile. "Mr. Frangione informed me you'd be arriving around this time."

"Oh?"

"He's currently in a meeting. Do you mind waiting here? It shouldn't be too much longer, then you can go upstairs."

"Sure." I backtracked to her desk. "Are you a regular at Nails R Us?"

Startled, she looked down at her hands and then back at me. "Excuse me?"

"The butterfly on your nails." I explained. "It's done in their special colour."

Her chocolate eyes widened. "You knew the salon based on one colour?"

"It's a rather unique shade of blue."

"You have a great eye, Miss Baxter."

"Roxanne, please." I dug into my purse for a business card and pen. "If you want to try someplace, go to Dagger Designs. Hand this card to the receptionist, Lexi, and you'll receive a fifteen percent discount on a new set of nails."

"Seriously?" She took the card, eyeing it suspiciously. "Is this a scam?"

I put a hand to my chest, feigning hurt. "That'll be bad for business."

She took a closer look at the card. "You're the owner of Dagger Designs?"

"A pleasure to meet you." I extended my hand.

"Mercy." She clasped her hand in mine. "My name is Mercy."

"I hope to see you in my salon, Mercy."

"At least once." Mercy grinned, holding up my business card. "I can't let this discount go to waste."

I laughed. A ping on her computer drew her attention. Mercy informed me that Nico's meeting was finished, and I could go upstairs. I thanked her and turned away. The conversation with Mercy helped ease some of my nerves, but now that I'm heading to see Nico, my nerves are coming back.

Nico's office door was open. I stopped short at the door frame. A blonde woman in a white one-piece jumpsuit was leaning into Nico as he reviewed some papers. Jealousy curdled my stomach. She was beautiful. They looked good together. I knocked on the door frame.

Nico looked up, and when his eyes met mine, he smiled. "Bella."

It was that smile that had me smiling back. The jealousy inside unravelled into warmth. *He's mine. He picked me.* The blonde scowled at me and leaned in a little closer to Nico. I didn't let it bother me. Nico wasn't paying her any attention.

"Am I interrupting?"

"No." Nico put the papers he was reviewing down. "Paige. I need you to collect all the data from the past six months. I'll review it all when I return from lunch."

"Of course, Nico. I'll be happy to review it with you." She batted her eyes.

"That won't be necessary." Nico stated dismissively.

The woman, Paige, pursed her red lips, turned on her heels and stormed past me. I felt rather smug that he completely ignored her. Though, there was a niggling in the back of my mind that warned me not to piss her off again. The warning slipped away when Nico's fingers gently turned my face to him. Then his lips found mine in a soft caress, and all I could think about was him.

"Ready?"

It took me a moment to re-orient myself. "As ready as I'll ever be."

He chuckled. "That's supposed to be my line."

Nico wrapped an arm around my waist and led me to the elevators. I raised a questioning brow as he hit the P button, but all he did was smirk, squeezing my side. The doors opened to underground parking. Nico led me to the blue car I was sitting in the first time I'd shown up at the dealership. Some man with brown hair that curled around his ears and square glasses leaned against the hood. He handed Nico the keys.

"What's going on?" I questioned, looking between the two men.

"I don't know where we're going for lunch." Nico dangled the keys in front of me." You'll have to drive."

"What's wrong with my car?"

The brown-haired man laughed. "I like her."

"So do I." Nico stated without losing eye contact with me. "Bella, do you not want to drive this car?"

My gaze slid to the car. I remembered the rumble of the engine when I turned it on last time. *I'll never get another opportunity.* I snagged the keys from Nico. The other man grinned and opened the driver's side door for me.

"Have fun." He winked before closing the door.

I started the engine and then adjusted the seat and mirrors. Nico slid in next to me. I waited for him to buckle up before leaving the underground parking. My smile grew as I picked up speed. *Apparently, I'm a speed junkie.* I went as fast as I dared not to get caught by any cops roaming the streets. It wouldn't be good if Dad or Tyler learned about it today. I don't want them to find out, at least not yet. It might put Mom in a precarious situation.

I drove us to a family-run diner on the other side of Frostham. Mom knows the owner. They went to high school together. Mom's friend's grandparents opened the restaurant. The food is fantastic. A few of the recipes haven't changed and are still the best sellers. The best part about the diner is that it's far away from the station. There's no way Dad, Tyler, or even Jaylen would find us here.

I parked away from the front door, hoping the distance would limit any accidental dings from other vehicles. Nico opened the restaurant's door for me. I couldn't move. I could only stare inside. Nico closed the door with a frown. He gently moved us aside so we wouldn't block the door.

"Bella, what's wrong?"

"I can't do this." I took a step back.

"Do what? Have lunch with your mom?"

"Introduce you to her."

He lifted my chin. "Are you embarrassed to be with me?"

"No. That's not it." I closed my eyes, shaking my head. "In a way, I've lied to Mom and betrayed the family. I know it's ridiculous. I can say a lot and put on a brave face when I'm away from my family. Now that it's right in front of me, just beyond those doors, I'm not sure I can go through with it."

"You have two options." Nico soothed, rubbing my arms. "We can leave right now, or we can go inside. Either option you choose, I will be following your lead."

I looked back at the diner door. If Mom disapproves of Nico, she could tell Dad, and then he'll arrest Nico just to separate us. Or Mom could become an ally and help me figure out how to convince Dad that Nico is not the Frangione he should be focused on. A family of five walked out of the restaurant. My gaze followed them to their car, the kids giggling as they ran ahead of their parents. My heart tightened. We used to be like that before Grandpa died. Nico's dad ruined that for us. He's the one my dad should be focusing on.

"Standing mom up will only make things worse for us."

"Very well." Nico kissed my forehead and then opened the door. "After you, Bella."

I took a deep breath and entered the diner. All the delicious scents hit me at once, and the familiarity of them eased my tension. Nico rested a hand on my back as I led him to Mom, who was already in a booth waiting for me. She looked up as we neared, her smile faltering when she saw Nico.

"Roxanne." Mom got up to pull me into a hug. "I was starting to think you wouldn't show."

"It crossed my mind." I mumbled. "This is Nico."

"It's a pleasure to meet you, Mrs. Baxter." Nico smiled, extending his hand.

"I know who you are, Mr. Frangione." She stated flatly.

"That would be my father. Please call me Nico."

Mom stared at his hand, her lips thinned. She then looked at me. I pleaded with my eyes for her to play nice, silently telling her that I needed this. Nico began to lower his hand when Mom extended hers. He grasped it and then leaned down to kiss the back. Mom pulled her hand away. I swear she would have wiped her hand if we weren't watching.

"Will you listen?" I questioned, ready to beg if necessary.

With a curt nod, we all slid into the booth. Nico leaned back casually, his arm draped across the back of the booth. He opened a menu that was on the table and began to peruse the options. I began my story, starting with how, or rather where, Nico and I met — telling her that Tyler did warn me about Nico and had me wear a wire during our first date. As the past two weeks came out in a rushed explanation, I began leaning into Nico, needing his silent strength as I continued.

The waitress came around to take our orders. Mom and I went to the diner so often we didn't need to look at the menu. I asked for the BBQ burger topped with sauteed mushrooms, BBQ sauce and a side of onion rings. Mom ordered the club with a green salad, while Nico ordered a bacon cheeseburger with fries. At the last minute, I ordered a caramel milkshake. Nico chuckled.

"What?" I turned to him.

"You like caramel drinks." He stated.

"I do." I smiled. "I might like caramel more than chocolate."

"Interesting."

Mom cleared her throat. "Why are you dating him?"

My cheeks heated. "Nico makes me feel... special."

"You are special, Bella." Nico leaned down to kiss my cheek.

"Any man can make you feel special." Mom prompted. "So why him specifically?"

"I don't know how to explain it right." I could feel my cheeks burning hotter. "When I'm with Nico, I feel strong, bold, and invincible. But I also feel vulnerable and protected. It's a whirl of emotions with Nico. It just feels right being with him."

Mom pinned Nico with a stern look. "Do you know about our family history?"

"Yes." Nico told her honestly. "Bella told me about it. I didn't want to, but I was willing to let her walk away."

"I stayed." I rested a hand on Nico's thigh. "I want to be with Nico."

Mom leaned back with a sigh. "I will make my final decision after lunch."

Mom then turned her attention to Nico, asking him standard get-to-know-you questions. We fell silent when the food came and took our first few bites. The burger was just as juicy and flavourful as it always is. I let out a soft little moan. Opening my eyes, I found both Nico and Mom smiling at me.

"What?"

"Oh, nothing." Mom said in a singsong manner.

"That's it." Nico proclaimed. "I'm taking you to every restaurant Frostham has to offer."

"Why?" I frowned at him.

"Because I want to see that pleasure-filled smile you get when you fall in love at first bite."

"You really don't have to do that."

"But I really want to." He grabbed my milkshake and took a sip.

"Hey!" I snagged my milkshake back.

Mom chuckled. I looked at her, startled. It's easy to forget others are around when I'm with Nico. Mom picked up the conversation. She interrogated Nico covertly, then flipped the questions to me. When I finished my milkshake, I needed to use the bathroom. Nico slid out, kissing me before letting me go. Coming out of the hall with the bathrooms, I bumped into one of the last people I wanted to see today.

"Jaylen." I was careful not to look past him to Nico.

"Hello, Roxanne." He smiled.

"What are you doing here?"

"Late lunch. They have the best onion rings in the city."

I nodded. "I should get back to my table."

Jaylen looked over the restaurant. "Who is your mom talking to?"

"Does it matter?" I said defensively.

"Just making friendly conversation."

I began to walk past him when he took hold of my elbow. I looked down at his hand with a frown. He slid it down to mine and squeezed.

"I'm sorry again about the cameras in your salon. You know Ty got them for your protection. He's worried Frangione is going to use you as bait or worse."

"All you had to do is ask." I said softly, unable to pull my eyes away from our connected hands. "I listened when you asked me to wear a wire."

"Rox, I want us to have a relationship."

I looked up at him. "No."

"It'll protect you from Nico Frangione." He insisted. "We're good together. I can make you happy."

"I don't need protecting, Jaylen."

I tried pulling my hand back, but he wouldn't let go. Jaylen tugged me forward, cupped the back of my neck and kissed me. Anger boiled inside. I itched to slap him but refused to make a scene. *Has Jaylen always been this persistent?*

"I won't give up on you." Jaylen rested his forehead on mine. "We are meant for each other."

Twenty

NICO

I watched Roxanne disappear down a hall toward the washrooms before I slid back into the booth. Jenna Baxter watched me. A penetrating stare that made me want to squirm, but I refused to give her any reaction. *This is a test.* I was reasonably sure she reserved that stare for the criminals she faced in the courtroom when she was a prosecutor. I am no criminal.

"What are your intentions with my daughter?"

I forced a lazy smile as I leaned back in the booth. "My intentions are simple. I want to date your daughter."

"Dating her has nothing to do with her father?"

"At first." I admitted.

Roxanne said I'd need her mother in my corner. Honesty will be the best way to do that. It won Roxanne over. It'll win her mother over.

"I wanted to seduce her to gather inside information more effectively."

Jenna's glare hardened, and her lips thinned. I knew she wouldn't like that answer, but I pressed forward. Leaning on my forearms, I kept eye contact so she could understand how serious I was.

"Instead, Roxanne seduced me. After our first date, I discovered the strength behind her beauty. I learned how protective she is of her friends, staff, and business. And she's loyal to her family." I paused to take a breath. "Roxanne is also soft, sweet, and vulnerable. I can sense she also wants to be happy. I want to make her happy. I want to be the only one she can trust enough to just be herself with. I want to see her smile and hear her laugh."

Jenna's gaze softened, but her lips remained a thin line. She didn't believe a word I was saying. I don't need her to believe me, but Roxanne wants her to. With that in mind, I refrained from telling her off. Barely. Roxanne's brother and father will be next to learn of our relationship, and they will be the hardest to convince that I've fallen for Roxanne Baxter.

"You know all the right words to say." Jenna accused.

I shrugged. Jenna Baxter may never be in my corner. She seems like the kind of mother that will do anything for her daughter.

"Have you considered what your relationship with my daughter will do to her relationship with her father?"

"I have." I nodded. "I've even told her I'll let her go. Yet here she is, wanting you to approve our relationship."

"What does Enzo Frangione want with my daughter?"

The question startled me. I leaned back with a scowl. Instinct has me not wanting to answer her. I hate how people assume I know what my father wants and what he's planning. Those are questions for Franco, not me. Jenna kept her gaze on me, observing my reaction. There is no point holding back now. I took a steadying breath but couldn't restrain the disgust in my tone when I did finally answer her.

"I won't let him go anywhere near Roxanne."

"That doesn't answer my question."

"The only thing I know is that he wants to know what the cops know." I gritted my teeth. "He wants whatever information Roxanne will spill."

"Will you give him insider information? Will you use my daughter?"

"Fuck him." I growled. "He can go burn in hell."

Jenna laughed. I blinked, confused by the sudden change in demeanour. She apologized as she tried to regain her composure.

"You're a contender to make my daughter truly happy."

I raised a brow. "Only a contender?"

"There's another." She jerked her chin, her eyes on a space behind me. "Someone else who could also make her happy. There are less complications with him."

I turned to see some brown-haired guy kissing Roxanne. Furry bloomed within. I clenched my jaw and fisted my hands. It took all my willpower not to march over and pull them apart and then punch the man. *Come one, Roxanne, push him away.*

The man pulled back, resting his forehead on hers. I turned away, unable to watch any longer. If it's the same man I saw her with last week, then it must be the friends-with-benefits guy she broke off with.

Roxanne returned to the table. "I'm sorry, Mom, we should get going."

"So soon?" Jenna queried.

"I have to get Nico back to work."

I reached into the breast pocket of my suit jacket to pull out my wallet. "Let me pay for lunch."

Jenna waved a hand in front of her face. "I've got this, you go."

"I insist." I pulled out a few bills, estimating how much was needed. "I interrupted your mother-daughter lunch."

"Very well." She slid out to hug Roxanne. "Have a good day, sweetheart."

"Love you, Mom."

"It was a pleasure meeting you, Mrs. Baxter."

"Jenna." She corrected. "You can call me Jenna, Nico."

I nodded. It was a step forward. With a hand on Roxanne's back, I guided her out of the restaurant and to the car. I opened the driver's door for her to slide in. She started the engine, waiting for me to buckle up before putting the car into drive. Roxanne was quiet for most of the drive. I itched to confirm my suspicions about the man and that kiss in the diner.

"You saw, didn't you?" Roxanne finally spoke.

"Who is he?" I blurted. "The one you kissed. Was that the man? You're friends-with-benefits that you broke off last week?"

If I hadn't shifted in my seat, I would have missed her nod. Roxanne was keeping her eyes on the road. Her white knuckle grip on the steering wheel had me wondering what was going through her mind. I need to tell her about Paige. She's told me about her recent sex partner. I need to tell her about mine.

"Do I need to be concerned?"

"About what?" She glanced at me, startled.

"About that man taking you from me?"

"No." She answered immediately.

We'd reached the dealership, and Roxanne pulled into the underground parking. She put the car in park, turned off the engine, and turned to me. Gripping my face in her hands, there was a seriousness in her eyes that had me holding my breath.

"I'm with you. He had me for a year and did nothing until I was with you." Roxanne told me. "I am yours, Nico."

I smiled. "Music to my ears."

She kissed me, the first one she's initiated. It was sweet, with just enough possessiveness to back up her claim of being mine. I still want to know who the man is so I can warn him away from Roxanne. For now, I'll settle on this moment. Her light pushes the darkness within me away, but I know it still lingers inside, and it doesn't take much for it to take over. I told Roxanne to find Marco and return the keys to him, the man whom she met before lunch. I let her off the elevator on the first floor and continued to my office.

I returned to my office. The documents I'd asked Paige to collect weren't there. It's not like her to be untimely. I looked over the railing to the sales floor but couldn't see her blonde head below. *Where is she?* Marco came up the stairs just as I turned to retreat to my office.

"How was lunch?"

"Interesting." I said mildly. "Did Roxanne catch you? I told her to give you the car keys."

"No." He looked over the railing. "There she is."

"Have you seen Paige?" I asked as he turned to head back down. "Paige was supposed to collect some data for me and have it on my desk by the time I got back."

"Ah. She's in the board room."

With a nod, I went down the hall. Sure enough, there was Paige. *How did I miss her?* The door was wide open, and she's not exactly a woman you'd miss in a crowd. I walked right past the boardroom. Paige sat on the table, her legs crossed, the zipper going down the front of her outfit was lowered to show off her cleavage. My eyes were drawn to the papers on the table, not to the women sitting on it.

"Is that the data I asked for?"

"Yes." She purred.

I moved forward. "You can leave now."

"Let me help you, Nico." Paige slid off the table and pressed into me. "It'll be a long night if you work alone."

"I can help." Roxanne's voice flowed from the doorway behind me.

"You're not an employee."

"No, I'm not, but I can keep my boyfriend company as he works."

"Boyfriend?" Paige let out a bitter laugh. "Nico doesn't do relationships."

"Strange." Roxanne mused. "Because he called me his girlfriend this weekend."

"Nico Frangione wouldn't date a woman like you."

Paige stood toe-to-toe with Roxanne. Both are beautiful women, yet different. Paige knows she's gorgeous and confidently shows it off. In contrast, Roxanne has a shy beauty about her that makes me want to dress her up and show her off.

"You mean smart?" Roxanne countered. "Thank you for the compliment."

I bit back a smirk. Paige crossed her arms under her breasts and towered over my girlfriend in her five-inch heels. The fire in Roxanne's gaze as she glared at Paige had my cock hardening. I need to get Paige out of the room so I can fuck my woman.

"I mean plain." Paige responded.

"Maybe that's exactly what he needs to get away from a harpy like you."

"When he leaves you like he's done plenty of other women, I'll still be here."

"At least you have standards, even if they are someone's seconds." Roxanne smirked.

"Bitch." Paige snarled, raising her hand to slap Roxanne.

"Paige." I growled through clenched teeth. "Leave."

She turned to me wide-eyed as if surprised I was there. A blush coated her cheeks, her mouth opening and closing like a fish. Unable to find any words, she snapped her mouth shut and hurried out of the room. I followed only to close and lock the door. Turning back to Roxanne, I couldn't wipe the smile from my lips. She stood there, arms crossed, and that fire still blazing in her eyes.

"That woman is haughty."

"She was my employee-with-benefits." I explained. "A decent fuck, but nothing more."

"You took her home?"

"Never. You're the first."

Roxanne nodded. "So we both have a past… lover."

"Fuck-buddy." I corrected firmly, stopping in front of her. "Speaking of fucking."

Roxanne blushed. "Don't you have work to do?"

"I'll get to it."

I twisted my fingers in her hair and kissed her hard. Roxanne melted into me, her arms wrapping around my neck. *I need to relieve the tension in my balls if I want a chance to concentrate on the task ahead.*

"Condom." Roxanne ordered.

I pulled one from my jacket pocket with a grin. Roxanne took a step back and peeled off her shirt. My eyes locked onto her breasts. She then shimmied out of her capri pants and hopped onto the table. *I'm never going to look at this table the same again.* With a seductive smile from Roxanne, I lunged forward. *I need this woman in my life forever. Maybe I need a ring.*

Twenty-One

ROXANNE

ALL DAY, I'VE BEEN waiting for the worst to happen. I was waiting for my brother or dad to scold me for being seen in public with Nico yesterday. Nothing came. Jaylen must not have told them about seeing me at the diner. I can only hope he doesn't know it was Nico having lunch with Mom and me, but I doubt that.

Just in case, I have been extra cautious when driving to Nico's place since he gave me a key yesterday. Paul, head of security at his condo building, wanted to meet me, so Nico made introductions. When Nico walked away to take a phone call, Paul told me that Nico had never done this for anyone before. That knowledge made me all warm, and I treated Nico with a special kind of thank you. Nico even encouraged me to keep things in his place. The more intimate Nico and I become, and it's moving fast, the more nerve-wracking it will be when Dad finds out.

Every Friday, Cluvus Schola tries to bring in a graduate from the school to talk about their experience. It's an excellent opportunity for the students to learn what is out there after receiving a certificate. Today, I've been asked to be a special guest speaker.

"Rox."

Ethan greeted me when I walked into the school. The gorgeous Greek god of a man is breathless. Dirty blond hair, green eyes, all muscles and no fat, and the smile he throws at people should come with a warning. Women around the world, and men too, become putty in his hands when he smiles. He's a very hard man to say no to. He's also the director of the school, single and completely straight. There was a time I considered asking him out, but he put me in the friend zone pretty quickly. He said he was thrilled to add another rare friend who can resist his charm. Yeah, he's got a bit of an ego, but I can't really blame him.

"Hey, Ethan." I smiled at him.

"Thank God I saw your car pull in from my office window."

"Oh?"

"Someone wants to be a donor to the school, but he just rubs me the wrong way."

"So you don't want his money?"

"Nope." He wrapped an arm around my shoulders. "Let me walk you to class before I'm forced back to my office."

"Heaven forbid you actually have to face this donor."

Ethan laughed, and his laughter put me in a good mood. That is until a dark cloud blocked my joy. Franco Frangione. He came down the stairs that I knew were at the end of the hall. A brief look of surprise crossed his features before he grinned at me. Nothing good will come from that grin. *Stay on guard.* I reminded myself.

"Playing the field farfalla?" He mocked. "How disappointing. It'll break my poor little brother's heart."

"What are you doing here, Franco?" My shoulders squared defensively.

"I came to donate some funds to this school, but the director would prefer to be in your company than talk money. Though I can't blame him, you are perfect company." Franco reached out, his fingers ghosting over my cheek. "I wonder if Nico's threat will hold any value after he learns about this."

"Touch me and find out." I challenged.

"Not today." He pulled his hand back and nodded at Ethan. "Another day, Mr. Grekko."

Neither one of us turned to watch Franco leave. When I suspected he was far enough away, or better yet – out of the building – I sagged into Ethan. The cops should be investigating Franco. The man gives me the creeps.

"Whatever he offers, don't take it." I told Ethan.

"You know him?"

"Unfortunately. He's my boyfriend's brother."

"Boyfriend?" Ethan questioned me in surprise. "Has the cop finally admitted his feelings for you?"

I winced. "He has, but he's not my boyfriend."

"I need details."

"I need to get to class."

Ethan laughed. "You can't avoid me, Rox, not in these halls."

"I can try."

He opened the door to the class I was to talk to today, and every eye in the room turned to us. Ethan gave me a little shove forward before closing the door. I smiled and waved. The instructor came to greet me and told me I was a little early. So I took a seat off to the side and let him finish the lesson he was working on, which was about French tips using acrylic. Twenty minutes later, after the students had a chance to try the techniques themselves, I was introduced to the class.

"Hi." I waved, looking at all the young faces in the room. "Either I'm getting older or interest in being a nail technician has grown with a younger generation."

That elicited a few giggles. I relaxed.

"As your instructor introduced, my name is Roxanne Baxter, and I own Dagger Designs. I went to school for business with the goal to open my salon, then came to Cluvus Schola. This school helped me to master the technique of sculpting acrylic nails. Before coming here, all I could do was paint awesome designs."

Someone raised their hand, and I pointed, permitting them to speak. "Was it hard starting your own business? Would you recommend it?"

"That's a trick question. Yes, starting my own business was very hard. A lot of money goes in at the start with not a lot of profit. It took about eight months before I started to see a profit." I paused to contemplate the second question. "Would I recommend starting your own business? I'm not sure. It's quite rewarding if you succeed, but there are a lot of salons in Frostham to compete with. On the other hand, I think you have to be a person who can persevere to be able to succeed. I highly suggest business classes if you want to open your own salon."

Someone else raised their hand. "How did you make your business stand out?"

"The name helped. I also used social media to my advantage to showcase the artistic style of my employees. We ensure every set of nails we build is perfect, and every client is satisfied."

Dahlia raised her hand. "Would you hire students from this school?"

"Of course." I smiled at her. "All of my nail technicians have a diploma from here. Before I hire them, their interview consists of doing my nails. I test the quality of their work for one week before deciding to hire them. In fact, I'm looking into opening a second location and would need to hire more nail technicians."

That caused an excited chatter to fill the room. I grinned, thrilled to see that kind of excitement.

"Okay, okay, settle down." I spoke loudly to quiet them. "I would only hire one or two students from this school."

Someone in the front raised their hand. "Most businesses like to hire those who have experience. How do we gain experience if no one hires us?"

"Ah, it's a vicious cycle. As I said, there are many salons in the city for you to apply to, and I know a few of them do hire recently graduated students from Cluvus Schola. When you apply, make sure you have a small portfolio of your work, whether a physical photo album or your social media album. It will highlight your talent."

"Can we see you in action?"

I looked to the instructor. He smiled and gestured to the work table. It is already set up with the supplies needed for French tip nails. A camera poised just above the workstation will record what I'd be doing and project it onto a screen for all the students to see without needing to crowd around. I took a seat, familiarized myself with what was set up, and placed everything where I wanted it to be.

"I'll show you how quickly a French tip can be completed in a workplace environment. Then I'll do a reverse French."

While placing a form on a dummy finger, holding it as I would a client, I reminded them about prepping the nail before starting any work. I talked through the process while working at the same speed as I do at Dagger Designs. The white tip is placed and formed first, ensuring the smile lines and points are perfect and checking down the barrel that the acrylic is thin. Then, the pink colour goes onto the nail plate and up against the top. It can not go over the top of the white, or else you'll lose the shape. A bead of clear acrylic is used in the center, drawn out over the colours to the edge for structure.

I looked up to see the enraptured faces of the students. It doesn't take long for the acrylic to dry. I tapped it lightly with my nail to check the dryness before removing the form and shaping the nail to a smooth almond shape. Taking another finger, I showed them the reverse. This time, I was starting with the pink on the nail plate and building it a little high. I shaped the smile line but removed the form to file the shape so it is nice and crisp. I explained the shape can be filed with the form in place, but removing it is better. Putting the form back on, after brushing away the dust, I layered on the white colour. I explained if some of the colour landed on the pink, it was okay because it would be filed away. Nail dry and filed, I placed them side by side under the camera and looked up.

"Can you tell the difference?"

I was met with open mouths and shaking heads. A chime went off, indicating the end of class. The instructor thanked me and told the students to have their lunch. Ethan waited for me in the hall, but it was the students who wanted my attention more. I was thanked as they left for lunch, and a few had more questions. Then there was only Dahlia.

"Yes, Dahlia?"

She looked nervous. "Would you hire me?"

"That's why I put you through." I told her. "I think you'll enjoy working at my salon over your aunts."

"She wasn't too happy when I told her about Cluvus Schola." Dahlia cringed.

"Your talent needs to be honed, which can't be done under the tutelage of family." I told her. "You have the skill, Dahlia. I want to see how much better you can be after some schooling."

"How come Aunt Carole never suggested this school?"

"She never came here." I shrugged. "Go have lunch. When you graduate, I want you to show off your diploma."

She nodded before peeling down the hall for lunch. Ethan threw an arm around my shoulders, guiding me to his office. He had lunch ordered in. There was no escaping his prying questions now, though I did try. By the end of lunch, he had gotten everything he wanted. The smile on his face and the laughter in his eyes indicated his amusement over my current love life.

During lunch with Ethan, Barbara had called. There was a cancellation, and her dress fitting was moved up. I swung by the salon to check in with Lexi and informed her of my change in afternoon plans. There was one client I had to do before running off. My staff can pick up the other three clients. Since Nico came into my life, Lexi has been reducing my client list. Thankfully, I have a new hire starting next week, and my realtor is looking into potential retail space for me to open a second location.

I was ten minutes late getting to the bridal shop. The receptionist told me that Barbara was already downstairs getting fitted. I made my way down, passing two other brides before reaching Barbara's fitting area. Her sister, Liz Larson, sat on the couch. She turned her caramel eyes my way as I approached.

"You're late." She stated matter-of-factly.

"This was last minute, and I had a client I had to work on before coming here." I responded. "I got here as fast as I could."

"Good, you're here." Barbara sounded relieved when the curtain pulled back. "What do you think?"

My mouth fell open. She looked stunning. The eggshell white wasn't too stark against her lightly tanned skin. The soft tool skirt billowed out from her waist to give her fairy-like movement. The bodice was covered in lace that trickled down into the skirt and covered the sleeves. It suited her curvy body perfectly. I loved it when she first tried it on. Now that the seamstress has pinned it in spots, it looks even better.

"Wow, Barb." I finally found my tongue. "It looks fantastic on you."

"Really?"

"I said this last time, and I'll say it again. Jonah will be left speechless."

Barb turned to her sister. "Liz?"

"You're stunning." She stood to examine the fitting, forcing the seamstress to step back. "It could be cinched at the waist more."

"I wouldn't use a great big vale." I added. "Maybe just a jewelled headband. We wouldn't want to overwhelm the dress."

"I don't want it cinched more." Barb complained, running her hands over her stomach. "What if I gain weight?"

"You still have two more fittings." Liz countered. "On the last fitting, you can cinch up, then you'll need to maintain that weight until you walk down the aisle."

Barbara cringed. I know her. This wedding is stressing her out, and with the stress comes a weight gain. Liz is right. It'll look even more perfect cinched up. Barb closed the curtain to change.

"Are you still bringing a plus one?" Barb asked through the curtain. "Rox?"

"That's the plan." I haven't talked to Nico about being my plus one, but I'm sure he'll accept.

"Have you not asked?"

"Not yet, but I'm not worried."

"Who are you bringing?" Liz questioned me. "Is it that cop you've been seeing?"

I bit the inside of my cheek. She'll find out while she's helping Barb with the finer details of the wedding planning, such as the place setting and wedding favours. This might put her in an awkward position at work. Liz is a prosecutor working with the police, just like my mom was. I know she's working on the Frangione case. There's no point in avoiding the question.

"It would be Nico." I finally said.

"Frangione? Nico Frangione?" Liz's eyes widened. "Why in the world would you get yourself tangled up with him?"

"He came out of nowhere, Liz, and took my heart. I didn't plan for him."

"Wait. Do you love him?"

Barb flung the curtain open. "Do you?"

"I don't know, maybe, I think so." I answered. "I haven't quite figured things out yet. It's complicated. I feel differently with Nico than I have with my past boyfriends."

"I don't need to hear this." Liz covered her ears. "It'll be a conflict of interest."

"I'm sorry." I winced. "But Nico is innocent."

"You're biased."

I bit my tongue. There's a lot about the case that I think the police have wrong, but it's not my place to say anything. She picked up her purse, squeezed my arm and left the fitting area. I listened to Liz's heels click on the laminate flooring as she briskly left. Barbara picked up her purse, and I followed her to a desk where she set up another appointment for a fitting. Then she looped her arm in mine, and we left the bridal salon.

"What's the conflict of interest that Liz was talking about?" She asked me.

"Liz is working with Ty, Jaylen, and others to build a case against Nico that my dad is spearheading." I explained. "They won't find anything. Nico is innocent of their accusations."

"I'm sorry." Barb leaned into me. "I didn't know Liz was working on a case against Nico."

"You're not supposed to know what cases she's working on."

"Actually, I didn't know there was a case against Nico."

I smiled bitterly. "I didn't know until after we met. Ty told me what they're accusing him of, but I don't believe any of it."

"Care to tell me?"

"Not happening." I shook my head, stopping at her car. "It's an active case. Technically, I shouldn't even know."

Barb shrugged. "I won't pry. Do you want to go out for drinks?"

I shook my head. "Thanks, but I think I'll surprise Nico with dinner tonight."

"Homemade?"

"Partially. I'm going to find myself an Italian grocery store and have a look around. Something is bound to inspire my cooking."

Twenty-Two

Nico

Today is the day. Today I'll buy Roxanne a ring. A perfect ring to fit her slender fingers. Except, I have no idea where to start, but Marco would know. With that in mind, I went to the dealership to talk to my friend. His advice will be well received. I have to get this right.

"Marco." I entered his office, closing the door behind me. "I need your help."

"Well, this will be good." He leaned back in his chair with a smirk. "What does the great Nico Frangione need help with?"

"How did you find the right ring for your fiancée?" I rubbed the back of my neck. "I'm assuming you bought her a ring before she asked you to marry her."

"I did." He said slowly, watching me. "Why do you ask?"

"I'm going to ask Roxanne to marry me."

Marco blinked. "You want to marry her?"

"That's what I said."

"You've only known her for a couple of weeks."

"I have." I said, not understanding his point.

"Have you thought this through?"

I glared at him, annoyed. "Yes."

Marco took in the information and leaned forward. "Explain this to me, Nico. I find it hard to believe that you've fallen so hard over a woman that your feelings for Rachelle pale in comparison."

"Rachelle left me. Roxanne is il mio ragglio di sole. She has me feeling things I never thought I'd feel again and more." I stared at Marco so he would understand how serious I was. "I love her, Marco. I want Roxanne to be my forever."

He studied me carefully. "She's your sunshine?"

"Yes."

"Wow." He leaned back in his chair. "I never thought I'd see the day when a woman finally gets you to live again. Rachelle really broke you."

I scowled at him. "Are you going to help me or not, Marco?"

He began to laugh. "Of course, I'll help you. That's what friends are for. Just promise me that I'll be your best man at your wedding."

"Only if she says yes."

I listened intently as he dove into an explanation of the colour, cut, and clarity of diamonds. Marco told me of the jeweller he used for a custom-made ring because nothing mass-market would suit his fiancée. It was a lot to take in, and

I was more uncertain about what kind of ring to get Roxanne after talking with Marco. The only thing I can do now is walk into a jeweller and hope to figure things out from there.

Roxanne would probably love receiving the famous blue box from Tiffany & Co. They are good quality, but still too mass-market for what I want. I ended up at Imperial Treasures. My mother received a ring from this jeweller, and so will Roxanne. I'd love to give Roxanne my mother's ring, but I don't want to ask my father for it.

I was greeted by a pretty redhead who, after learning why I was there, took me to a private room in the back. Shortly after, a clean-shaven man in a pressed dark grey suit entered. The room was simple, so the client and salesperson worked one-on-one. Only a desk and a computer sat in the room.

"Good day, sir. My name is George." He extended his hand with a warm smile. "How may I help you?"

"Nico Frangione." I stood, accepting his hand. "I'm here to customize an engagement ring."

He nodded. "Depending on the customization, it will take one to four weeks to create the ring."

I nodded my understanding. I'd have liked to present the ring to Roxanne as soon as possible, but I refused to give her something she could find anywhere. I can wait a little while to figure out the best way to propose. Hopefully, it'll only be a week until I have the ring in my possession.

"Do you have any idea as to how you'd like this ring to look?"

I shook my head. "It has to be one of a kind. I don't want anything that looks like it could have been purchased anywhere."

"That's what we do here at Imperial Treasures." George said patiently. "Let's start with the cut of the diamond."

He pulled a key from around his neck and unlocked a cabinet under the desk. I could only assume there was a hidden safe under there. George placed a black velvet tray with various diamond shapes on the desk in front of me. I didn't realize a diamond could be cut in so many different ways. Marco only listed a few of the cuts. One cut, though, stood out to me. It reminded me of the shape of her nails.

"That one." I pointed to it.

"Pear shape. Quite popular, it gives a slimming illusion to any finger." George explained. "The tip, though, would be its weakest point. If your fiancée does a lot with her hands, then may I suggest the oval."

"No, pear shape is the one for her."

"Very well." He typed something into the computer. "Do you want a coloured diamond?"

"I'm only aware of blue, pink, and yellow." I told him.

"Diamonds come in all colours of the rainbow." He changed the tray to one filled with colourful gemstones. "Lift them to the light. You'll see the colouring better."

I did as instructed. Purple, black, red, orange. Every colour of the rainbow, and even the in-between colours, sat on the tray. My eyes were drawn to the blue diamonds. Carefully holding four of them, I lifted them to the light. As beautiful as the clear blue diamond is, I rather like the one with a hint of grey in it. It would match Roxanne's eyes beautifully.

"This one." I held out the selected coloured gem.

"Greenish blue. Such a unique shade." George added the information to the computer. "What kind of metal do you want to use for the band? Sterling silver, yellow, rose, or white gold?"

"Would I be able to see the silver and white gold against the gem?"

"Of course, Mr. Frangione."

He pulled out two bands. I placed them on my finger, with the gem in the middle.

"The sterling silver does look better with the gem, but it requires frequent polishing to maintain its shine. It's also a softer metal and would mark up easily." George explained. "The white gold would need maintenance every few years, and it's much more durable."

"White gold, then."

"This is the last decision."

George pulled out another tray. There were too many options on how the bank could look. This took the longest time to decide. It couldn't be too thin or too thick, or it wouldn't be suitable for the shape of the diamond. In the end, I chose a filigree design that compliments everything I've chosen so far. For a final touch, I decided to have the inside of the band engraved. George showed me a 3-D version of all my choices on the computer.

"It's perfect." I concluded.

"I'll send the design to our craftsmen. It'll be done in one to two weeks. We'll call you when it's ready for pick up."

I provided him with all my information, including Roxanne's ring size, and then followed him to the front to pay. Franco was wandering the sales floor. *What is he doing here?* My brother grinned when he saw me and sauntered over.

"My little brother in a jewellery store." He teased. "I wonder who you could be buying for."

"You have no one to splurge on." I countered. "What are you doing here, Franco?"

"I'm looking for a gift for our sister."

"Candi's birthday is months away."

"No time like the present to start looking."

I doubt that, but I chose not to comment. I handed George my credit card as he rang me up. Franco gave a low whistle at the price.

"That's some piece of jewellery for someone so un-loyal to you."

My shoulders stiffened. "What are you talking about?"

"I saw her today." Franco said proudly. "She had another man's arm around her, and she was smiling."

I wasn't sure what to make of Franco's statement. I took my credit card back and left Imperial Treasures. Franco followed me out, continuing his one-sided conversation.

"I hope you didn't buy an engagement ring because I think Roxanne is playing you."

"She's not that kind of person."

"Are you sure about that? She rather enjoyed the kiss I gave her. Then you showed up."

I clenched my fists.

"Her little moan was quite addictive. I can see why you want to keep her around. As the daughter of a cop, she'd know how to manipulate you." He said, goading me.

"You need to stay out of my business, Franco." I snarled.

"Fine." Franco held up his hands. "I was only trying to help you, little brother. You fell hard for Rachelle. I just wanted to save you the heartache with Roxanne."

Fury coloured my actions. I spun fast and punched Franco. Rachelle left because of our father, Franco, who has no right to bring her up. Roxanne is nothing like Rachelle. I will not let him bad mouth her. Roxanne said she's mine, and I believe her. If Franco saw her with someone, then there must be an explanation.

"Stay away from Roxanne." I growled.

He chuckled. "You're weak, Nico, and she's your weakness."

He's right. Roxanne is my weakness. I slammed the car door shut and drove away from Franco's smug face.

Roxanne was already in my penthouse when I returned home. Cooking. She wore over-the-ear headphones, and her honey-blonde hair was tied up in a ponytail. It bounced as she danced around the kitchen. I smiled as I watched her. Roxanne didn't seem to notice I was home. Careful not to startle her, I moved closer and pulled out my phone to record the scene. *I'm not passing on this opportunity.* The song must have changed because Roxanne began humming, slightly out of tune but still cute, and her dancing became more enthusiastic. My smile widened. I love how comfortable she is in my place, with me. Roxanne spun on her toes like a ballerina. When she stopped, she was facing me, let out a shriek and put a hand to her chest.

"Nico!" Roxanne lowered her headphones.

"Bella."

"You scared me. How long have you been standing there?"

"Not long." I turned off the recording and returned the phone to my pocket.

Roxanne narrowed her eyes. "You were recording me?"

"For prosperity's sake." I moved in to pull her into my arms.

She grabbed a towel from the counter and threw it at me. "Delete it."

I laughed. *No way am I deleting it.* I wrapped Roxanne in my arms and kissed her. She kissed me back, all irritation vanishing. I love how she melts so willingly into me. A beeping had Roxanne pushing away. She turned to the oven, turned it off, then reached for a spoon and dipped it into a pot of red sauce.

Roxanne turned to me with the spoon outstretched. "Try this."

I leaned forward, wrapping my lips around the spoon. Wonderful flavours exploded on my tongue. "Delicious."

"Good." She tossed the spoon in the sink. Go freshen up. Dinner is ready."

"Come desideria, amore mio."

Roxanne sucked in a breath. "Nico."

I gave her a hard kiss. "I'll be right back."

Roxanne turned back to the stove, and I retreated to my bedroom. I returned my suit jacket to my closet numbly. I just called Roxanne, my love. I haven't used that term in years, not since Rachelle. Migrating to the bathroom, I splashed water on my face. *When did I start to love Roxanne?*

I gripped the sink's edge and stared at my reflection. Love is dangerous. Love will break me. Franco already knows Roxanne is my weakness. I have to put that ring on her finger before he uses her against me. My brother and father may be bastards, but they know to draw the line at wives and children.

I'll ask her to marry me tonight, even without the ring. Resolve made, I wiped my face and returned to see that Roxanne had already filled the table with the food she made. She finished pouring a glass of red wine, looked up and smiled. I don't deserve her, but I need her.

"Come sit." Roxanne gestured to the chair opposite her. "Before it gets too cold."

I took a seat at the dining table and surveyed the spread. Roxanne made spaghetti and meatballs with garlic bread. It smelled divine. It is a perfect setting for a marriage proposal.

"I hope you like it."

I looked up to see her blushing. "If it tastes as good as it smells, I'll be happy."

223

Her smile was tentative. "I hope so."

We served ourselves and began to eat. I already knew the red sauce was delicious. The meatballs were tender and well-seasoned. The pasta even tasted homemade. It was all delicious. I couldn't stop eating.

"So, it's good?" Roxanne questioned with a little laugh.

"Absolutely delicious. I can't remember the last time someone cooked for me."

"I know it's not fancy."

"It's perfect." I interrupted her. "Did you make the pasta yourself?"

Roxanne shook her head. "I found an Italian grocery store that makes and sells fresh pasta. I made the meatballs and garlic butter for the store-bought bread. The sauce is mom's. She had some frozen. All I did was thaw it out."

I reached across the table to take her hand. "I'll have to thank your mom. The red sauce makes the meal."

She laughed. We continued to eat. We talked about our day. Roxanne told me about her talk at the nail school but seemed a little tense, as if she was hiding something from me.

"I saw Franco today." Roxanne stated after we'd cleared the table.

"You went to Obsidian?" I tensed, already knowing that Franco saw her today.

"No, he was at Clavus Schola."

"The nail school? What was he doing there?"

"Apparently, he wanted to talk to Ethan about donating to the school." Roxanne put the remaining food into containers. "I told him not to accept any money from Franco."

"Who is Ethan? Why would he listen to you when it comes to the school?" Too many questions filled my mind. "Did Franco touch you?"

"No, Franco didn't touch me. Your threat from the party still lingered." She smiled, placed a pot in the sink, then turned to kiss my cheek. "Thank you."

I don't think it's the threat that held him back, but at least he kept his hands to himself. Franco is a calculating man. Crossing paths with Roxanne was planned. I only wish I knew why.

I frowned, realizing she hadn't mentioned anything about this Ethan person. "Bella, who is Ethan?"

"He's the director of the school." Her turn to frown. "He's just a friend, nothing more."

I pulled Roxanne into my arms and kissed her. "Just a friend?"

"He's a Greek god." Roxanne wrapped her arms around my neck. "You're my dark knight."

"I'm far from a knight."

"No." She agreed, sliding her hand down to my chest to where the tattoo was inked on my skin. "You're a dragon. Loyal and protective of what's yours. You'll reign fire down on anyone who crosses you."

She's got that right. Franco is wrong. Roxanne isn't my weakness. She's my strength. I love Roxanne Baxter. I will protect her from Franco and my father no matter the consequences. Franco's trip to the nail school unnerved me. He can get to her anytime, anywhere. Taking Franco off the board will increase Roxanne's safety, but any move I make, he'll see from a mile away.

Soft lips pressed against mine, and I focused on the woman in my arms. My woman. Hopefully, my wife. Those hazel eyes of hers looked at me concerned.

"Where did you go?" She asked.

"Nowhere that you need to be concerned yourself with."

"Are you sure?"

"Yes."

She looked at me skeptically but didn't pry. Roxanne squirmed out of my arms to do the dishes, but I stopped her. She made supper. I'll do the dishes. Then I'll show her how much I appreciate her cooking, and then, in the thralls of passion, I'll ask her to marry me. A smile curved my lips at all the things my mind conjured.

"What's that smile for?" Roxanne picked up the clean pot to dry and put away.

"What smile?" I teased my cock hard from my imagination alone.

"The one you're wearing."

My smile widened. "I'm just imagining all the ways I'm going to thank you for dinner."

She blushed. "And how many ways have you thought up?"

"Too many for one night."

Her blush deepened. I chuckled. She's adorable when flushed.

"We'll start with four. Then, after a rest, maybe two more."

She swallowed hard. Remembering how turned on she gets from dirty talk. I decided to tease her.

"I'll begin with that pretty mouth of yours." I explained, keeping a straight face while focusing on washing the dishes. "Then I'll move on to your breasts until you're begging. I'll have you coming on my tongue, my fingers, and my cock before I move onto the second way to thank you."

I glanced over at her. Her eyes widened, and her breathing picked up. She looked as though she was struggling to stand straight. I'd bet anything she was already wet. I took my time washing the dishes and continued the dirty talk. Roxanne was whimpering by the time I was done.

Screw it. I couldn't wait. I took Roxanne hard and fast on the dining table. She was soaked, and I was painfully hard. I barely had the brain cells to remember a condom before sliding into her. A proposal can wait. Right now, I need to fulfill every dirty promise I'd just made.

Twenty-Three

ROXANNE

"Good night, Roxanne, Lexi."

"Night, Rita." We called after her.

I waved as the final employee passed my office on her way to the back exit. She started a few days ago and has been doing really well in Dagger Designs. Lexi trailed after her to lock up. Then, she joined me in my office. I like to keep the hours of my business reasonable, closing at seven during the week so my staff can enjoy the rest of their night with their families. Friday and Saturday, we're open later to accommodate the demand. Closing earlier also means that Lexi and I won't be staying behind too late in the night with the sanitizing procedure we created.

"Okay." Lexi tucked a chair closer to my desk. "What do we have?"

"I've been reviewing all the properties the realtor sent over." I handed her over six of the property listings. "I've narrowed it down to these."

Lexi carefully went through the papers. "You'd have to see these locations to know if they'll work for the business."

I turned the computer screen so she could see better. "The realtor sent links. These are a few pictures of the inside."

"Hmm." She leaned forward and clicked through. "Probably doesn't do these places justice."

"No." I agreed. "Do you want to visit all the properties?"

"Let's pick three." Lexi shook her head. "Six is too many."

We went over the potential properties that I'd narrowed down from the dozen the realtor sent me. Dagger Designs has become so popular that a second location is needed. Lexi helped with decorating and staff hiring when I opened this location. For the second location, I want her to be more involved. I haven't brought it up yet, but I want to add her to the ownership.

Lexi and I worked on the pros and cons of each property based on the information we have. We pushed two properties aside after much debate due to their distance from Frostham's center. Down to four locations, we couldn't agree on which one to veto from the list.

"We're never going to agree." Lexi leaned back, stretching her arms over her head. "Just view all four."

I nodded. "When do you want to go?"

"Me?"

"Yes, you. I'd like you to be a co-owner."

"Me?" Her voice went up an octave. "Are you sure?"

"I am. You've done so much since the beginning. With the new location, I'll need the help, and I want to share the joy of ownership with you."

Lexi stared at me. I was suddenly second-guessing my decision. Maybe I should have asked instead of assuming she'll want to be a co-owner. When we talked about the business back in college, she said she only wanted to be an employee. I'd hoped that time might change her mind.

"I haven't made any changes." I backpedalled.

"No." Lexi rushed to assure me. "It just surprised me."

"So?" I hesitated. "Do you want to be a co-owner?"

"Yes." She beamed.

I grinned at her, pleased she wanted to join me in ownership. On paper, my mom is a partner in the business. By setting it up that way, it'll be easy to add Lexi. For now, I sent an email to the realtor and my lawyer to set up appointments for Lexi and myself.

"Business is done." I declared, turning off the computer and standing. "Let's get out of here."

"Co-owner." Lexi mused. "It won't be too much work to do that, will it?"

"Nope, we'll split the responsibility." I looped my arm around hers, walking to the breakroom for her to collect her things. "Now, stop talking about work. I want to know how your date went last night."

Lexi cringed.

"That bad?"

"He was so boring."

I frowned. "Was this the guy who you said was charming in all your back-and-forth messages? Or was this the one who sent you funny memes?"

"The charmer."

"What happened?"

"He's a journalist for the local paper. When he's writing, he has such a way with words." Lexi sighed. Hoisting her purse onto her shoulder, she looped her arm back with mine. "In person, his voice was dull and monotone. I nearly fell asleep in my soup as he talked about the article he was writing about."

"Maybe you should get off the dating apps and take a break." I suggested. "That's, what, the sixth bad date in two months?"

"Seventh." She corrected. "And it's been three months of bad dates."

I locked the back door to Dagger Designs. "I bet if you stopped trying so desperately to meet 'the one,' he'd find you unexpectedly."

When I turned back to Lexi, she wore a suspicious, shy expression. It took me a moment to read its meaning. With a gasp, I grabbed her shoulders and shook her lightly.

"Who was it?"

"What are you talking about?" Lexi stepped back, avoiding my gaze.

"You've met Mr. Right." I declared. "Who was he? When did you meet? How did you meet? I need details, Lexi."

She fidgeted, purposefully avoiding my gaze. "He was charming, funny, and attentive when I talked. It was only one night."

"Who was it?" I poked her side. "Who has stolen your heart, Lexi Dawson?"

She clamped her mouth shut. I repeated the question, poking her side. Lexi squirmed away, laughter bubbling up between us. It didn't take long for me to get Lexi to confess. Her sides are ticklish and, therefore, her weak spot.

"Okay." Lexi grabbed my wrists, stopping my next poke. "Okay."

"Who stole your heart?" I demanded.

"It was Tyler." She paused. "Baxter."

"What was me?"

I peered beyond Lexi to see my brother. His eyes were on Lexi, I looked back at Lexi. Her face turned bright red, and her eyes went wide as she stared at me. I couldn't tell if he overheard us or if he really wanted to know what we were talking about. Either way, Lexi is clearly embarrassed.

"What are you doing here, Ty?" I glared at my brother.

"I was just driving by and saw the two of you." Tyler gestured over his shoulder to indicate his idle car. "Lexi, I don't see your car. Do you want a lift home?"

Lexi bent her head, covering her face with her hands. That would be a no.

"We have a girls' night planned." I lied. "I'm her ride."

"Okay." He kept his eyes on Lexi, looking almost disappointed. "Have a good night."

"Night Ty."

"Night." Lexi mumbled.

Tyler turned to leave, stopped, and turned back around. "I'll have someone by this week to remove those cameras."

"Really?" I asked, hopeful.

"Yes, Rox, really. Cameras are useless with you covering them up all the time." He sighed, running a hand through his hair. "I'm sorry."

With that, he left. I urged Lexi to my car, which was only a few short steps away. I tucked her into the passenger side, got in behind the wheel and drove away from the salon. Lexi stayed silent the whole time.

I got Lexi into her apartment and settled on the couch before I got to work. First, I sent Nico a text to let him know I'll be at Lexi's tonight. I wish I could be with him tonight, but this takes priority. He replied, wishing us a good night. Next, I collected the Haagen-Dazs brownie cookie dough ice cream and two spoons. Sitting on the couch, legs crossed and facing Lexi, I offered her a spoon and dug in.

"Mmm. You always have the best ice cream." I shimmied.

"It's my cure to bad dates." She took a spoonful.

"I want to know exactly how you and Tyler met."

"I didn't know he was your brother." She insisted.

"Lexi, I don't care." I soothed. "I don't control what he does or who he does. The part I care about is you. I want to understand why you're not pursuing whatever it is you feel for him."

"He's your brother."

I pointed at her using my spoon. "Ignore that and start from the beginning."

Lexi took a mouthful of ice cream before speaking. "It was the night before Dagger Designs grand opening. My date had stood me up, so I was at a bar drinking alone when Tyler sat at the bar next to me. He called me beautiful and said I looked like I needed someone to talk to. We just hit it off. We talked and drank. He was easy to talk to, and we flirted."

I stayed quiet, afraid if I said anything, then Lexi might stop talking.

"He invited me to his place." Lexi glanced at me briefly before stuffing her face with ice cream.

"Don't stop now." I urged.

"It was the best sex of my life." She blurted out. "You know I slept around while in college, but none of that compared to sex with Tyler. Even now, no other man has been able to match Tyler in bed."

I inwardly cringed. This is information I didn't really need to hear about my brother. Lexi's face lit up when she talked about him, and I couldn't help but smile.

"We cuddled, talked some more, had more sex. In the morning, we took a shower together, ate breakfast, then parted ways. It wasn't until the grand opening that we saw each other again. I thought he had tracked me down until you introduced us." Lexi's demeanour saddened. "I knew I couldn't have a relationship with him after that."

"Why not?"

"He's your brother."

"So?" I scoffed.

"Wouldn't it have been awkward for you?"

"Yes, but you would have been happy, and I'd get used to it."

"What if we broke up?" Lexi came up with another excuse. "I'd still end up seeing him. Or maybe that would have ruined our friendship."

"What about now, after all these years?" I questioned her. "Would you be willing to follow your heart and go after Tyler?"

"I don't know." She poked her spoon into the ice cream.

"I think you should."

"What if I was just a one-night stand and the connection I felt was only one-sided? Besides, it's been so long."

I stuck my spoon into the half-eaten container and sighed. "That day, at the grand opening, I overheard a conversation between Tyler and Jaylen."

"What kind of conversation?" Lexi asked tentatively.

"Jaylen was asking if Tyler got lucky going to the bar the night before. Tyler responded with a yes."

"That's it?"

I shook my head, closing my eyes and drawing on the memory. "He said: Ditching you was the best decision I could have made. Jaylen teased him, but Tyler sounded serious in his answers. He said: The woman was more than a good fuck. I felt a connection with her."

"He really said that?" Lexi sounded doubtful.

I opened my eyes. "I'll never forget it. Tyler always joked around with his friends about the woman they slept with — conversations I was never supposed to overhear. But I really wanted to meet this woman that he spoke of. It seemed as though Ty never pursued her, and I got really busy with Dagger Designs. Now that I think about it, Ty hasn't been with a woman in years."

"How would you know?"

I shrugged. "It's how he holds himself when he's dating. I don't know how to explain it."

"Thanks, Rox."

"I mean it, Lexi. If Tyler's the one you can't forget, then go after him."

Lexi smiled softly. "Maybe I'm the idiot for waiting so long."

"You're only an idiot if you don't do as I say."

Lexi laughed.

I took the tub of ice cream and stood. "You pick a movie, and I'll order pizza."

Twenty-Four

NICO

WAKING UP WITHOUT ROXANNE in my arms is lonely and cold. I didn't realize how much of my heart she's taken until this moment. As I'm getting ready for work, Roxanne called.

"Buongiorno amore mio."

Roxanne sighed dreamily. "Morning Nico."

"What was that sigh for?"

"I love it when you speak Italian."

I smiled. "You also love it when I talk dirty."

"Mmm." She mused. "That's a very close second."

"Maybe I'll combine the two next time you're over."

"Promises, promises."

I grinned. "How was your night with Lexi?"

"After some girl talk, we watched movies and ate pizza. I really enjoyed our night."

"That's good." I locked up my apartment. "I'm about to step into the elevator. I may lose you."

"You'll never lose me." Roxanne teased.

"You're mine forever, Bella."

She giggled. "Aside from wanting to hear your voice this morning, I wanted to tell you that Ty is going to have the cameras taken down."

"That's good news. Should we celebrate?" I asked, opening the ring box I had picked up last night from Imperial Treasures. It's perfect. "There's actually something I have to tell you."

"Oh, sorry, Nico, I have to go. My lawyer is calling."

Roxanne hung up on me. I stared down at my phone. *Lawyer? Why does she need a lawyer?* Unease knotted my gut. Maybe asking her to marry me was too presumptuous of me. I hope she's not discussing ways to protect herself while she helps her brother put me behind bars. I shook my head at the ridiculous idea. Roxanne's not the type of person who'd do that. She's strong-willed and goes after what she wants. If she didn't want to involve herself with me, she wouldn't have.

There was an above-average number of customers in the dealership today. I came out of my office to help with sales. Except, there were no sales, only male customers looking around.

Something about today seemed off. When it was getting close to lunchtime, I slipped away to call Roxanne.

"Hello?" She answered without her usual cheer.

"Bella, do you want to have lunch?"

"Sorry Lexi, can you hold down the fort a little longer? Dad's making his put-the-phone-down-this-is-a-serious-conversation look."

Her father? That would explain why she called me Lexi. She must not have told him about me yet. If I'm going to propose, she'll have to tell him about us as long as she says yes.

"Is everything okay?"

"I'll talk to you later, promise."

With that, she hung up on me. For the second time today. First, the lawyer, now her father. I can't shake the feeling that something is going on. There was a commotion happening downstairs that drew my attention. I came out of my office to see a police raid. *What the fuck?* I could only stare as Detectives Baxter and Parry made their way up the stairs and put me in handcuffs. They then carted me through my place of business.

Anger settled in when I was placed in the back seat of a blue sedan, just like the one that followed me the day of the BBQ. Neither detective spoke as they drove to the station. Other officers glared at me as the detectives paraded me through the station. Out of the corner of my eyes, I saw her. Roxanne. When I turned my head, her wide eyes met mine for a moment. Captain Baxter forced her head into his chest to avert her gaze. I swear a look of horror flashed on her face when she saw me.

I was taken to an interview room. Removing the handcuffs, they drew my arms forward and handcuffed me to the table. My heart didn't want to believe that Roxanne betrayed me, but my mind couldn't let the thought go. She could have lied to me and was actually with her brother last night to plan this. That could be why she didn't warn me of the raid today. I shook my head. She might not have known about the raid. My heart and mind fought with the contrasting variations of the situation. Roxanne being here when I'm cuffed wasn't a coincidence.

"Finally." Detective Baxter sat across from me. "We have you."

"Have me on what?" I countered.

"Drugs, missing persons, murder. Which one do you want to go to jail for? My pick is all three."

Cristo. What has my family been doing? I refused to show any emotion toward the detective. They have no solid proof that I'm the one they are looking for. I might be able to gather information in this less-than-favourable position.

"You definitely have the wrong man." I argued.

"I don't think so, Mr. Frangione." Detective Parry smirked. "We have insider information. Very credible."

Again, my gut tightened. The way he worded that made me think of Roxanne. Could she have played me for a fool? Use me before I could use her. I've barely known her for a month. She could be an excellent actress. No. Her reactions to me were too honest to be faked. Damn, Franco, for putting a tiny seed of doubt in my mind.

"What we want to know is where you were two nights ago." Baxter drew my attention back to him.

"At home. Security cameras can prove that." I answered.

"Alone?"

"Does it matter? You won't believe anything I say."

"Were you alone, Mr. Frangione?"

"Yes." I refuse to drag Roxanne into this.

Tension eased from both men's shoulders. I can't tell if they were relieved I was alone so that their claims against me would stick easier. Or they don't want Roxanne tangled in this.

"Things will go a lot easier if you stay honest with us." Baxter pulled out a picture from a file folder he'd picked up while his partner brought me to this room. "Do you recognize her?"

I picked up the picture of Roxanne he'd placed on the table. He knew the answer, and I know he knows. I stared at Roxanne's smiling face. The image was cropped, and I wanted to know who she was smiling at. She looked happy and carefree and beautiful.

"What about these women?"

He then laid out half a dozen other pictures. All these women looked similar to Roxanne. Whether it was their blonde hair, hazel eyes, or the shape of their nose, some part of them drew images of Roxanne to mind.

"How long did you string them along?"

My hand tightened on the picture of Roxanne. Anger rising. *What the fuck is Franco doing?*

"I don't know them." I answered through gritted teeth.

"Really?" Parry questioned, doubtful. "They have a resemblance to the woman you're fucking around with."

My eyes fly to the detective. His green eyes glared at me from the other side of the table. He leaned against the mirrored glass with his arms crossed to show off his muscles and purposely be intimidating. That comment sounded personal.

"I'm not fucking around with anyone." I shot back.

"Then who is that going into Croquette with you?"

I looked down to see that Baxter pulled out another picture. A clear shot of Roxanne and me on our first date, my hand around her waist as we exited the restaurant. It must be the same shot that my Father had mentioned.

"You already know who that is." I countered. "As you did convince her to wear a listening device."

Parry's glare intensified. "Why did you take her out?"

"She's beautiful." I kept my gaze locked on his.

"It had nothing to do with who she is?"

I nodded. "She's an intelligent, strong, and bold woman. It makes her even more attractive."

Parry's jaw tightened. "What did you blackmail her with?"

"Excuse me?" The question took me back.

"What did you blackmail her with? There's no way she freely agreed to a date with you."

"But she did. No blackmail required."

"She was dating someone else at the time." He bit out.

"Jaylen." Baxter snapped.

Jaylen Parry glared at his partner before storming out of the interrogation room. I stared at the door. He must be the friends-with-benefits that Roxanne recently broke off. I didn't get a good look at him at the diner. His head was tucked down, and his lips were on my woman. Now that I think about it, he could be the man who took her out for lunch the day I had swung by Tina Toys. It's too bad he didn't realize what he had before she left him.

"Did you know her family connections before you asked her out?" Baxter drew my attention back to him.

"No." I answered honestly.

"Are her family connections the reason why she hasn't disappeared like the others?"

"No." I gestured to the pictures. "I don't know these other women."

"They were all at your club, Obsidian."

"Not my club." I told him. "Ownership belongs to my brother, Franco."

"Not according to the city records." Baxter pulled out another picture. "Do you recognize this man?"

I picked up the image of the clean-cut, family-looking man. "No."

"How about now?"

The following picture was of the same man but with longer hair, looser jeans, and a flannel shirt open over a t-shirt. At a glance, they look like two different people, but their eyes are the same. He must be an undercover cop.

"My answer is the same. I don't know this man."

Baxter scowled. "He was working for you, Mr. Frangione. Helping you with your drug operation. Two nights ago, he went missing."

"I'm sorry I can't help you."

"We want our officer back." Baxter pulled out a picture of the man in uniform. "Where is he?"

I was right. "I don't know. I have nothing to do with this. You have the wrong Frangione."

Just then, the door flew open to the interview room. A furious Roxanne stormed into the room. If this were an animated show, then I would have seen flames in her eyes and her hair flying around her head. She glared down at me, hands on her hips, shook her head once, then turned to her brother. *What did I do to earn her ire?* Behind her, Parry stood ready to pull her out. He must have sensed that she shouldn't be touched right now.

"Rox, you're interfering with an official interrogation." Baxter told his sister.

"You're interrogating an innocent man." She countered.

"He's a Frangione." Baxter growled at her. "He's not innocent."

"Sheep." Roxanne muttered.

Baxter stood, anger evident in the tightening of his muscles. "What did you say?"

"Bella." I tried to warn her.

Roxanne ignored me, poking her brother in the chest. "You're a sheep. You're blinded by the hatred your captain has for the Frangione name. He's the shepherd, and you're the sheep."

"Roxanne, get out before I have you arrested for interfering with a police investigation." Baxter warned.

"Bella." I tried again. "Listen to him, I'll be fine."

"A real detective would follow the evidence." Roxanne continued, ignoring all the warnings. "Nico is innocent of the crimes you're accusing him of."

"Jaylen!" Baxter ground his teeth.

The detective stepped forward, his hands placed on her arms. A growl rumbled out of me. Parry glanced at me. A ghost of a smile curled his lips.

"Take my sister to the cells to cool off."

Jaylen's hands tightened, tugging her back. "Come on, Rox."

Panic swirled with anger. Roxanne shouldn't be put behind bars, even temporarily. I also really wanted to punch Detective Parry for touching my woman. I couldn't figure out how to stop what was happening with me bound to a table.

"I was with Nico two nights ago." Roxanne declared.

The tension in the room because of the statement was palatable. All three of us looked at her. I couldn't believe she said that. I was trying to protect her.

"Bella, why would you say that?"

"Because it's the truth." She looked at me, eyes softening. "Ti amo."

Those two tiny words changed everything. *She loves me. My woman said she loves me, in Italian, in front of her brother.* I couldn't believe her bravery. A feeling of rightness settled inside. When I propose, I know she'll say yes.

"He couldn't have been with you all night." Parry countered. "He could have slipped out to make a call while you slept."

Roxanne turned her head and smiled sweetly. "I didn't get much sleep."

"Get her out of here." Baxter ordered.

Jaylen dragged Roxanne out of the room. He looked pissed and hurt. I felt warmth spread in my chest. I won Roxanne's love. When the door closed, Baxter glared at me.

"I'm putting you in a holding cell while I confirm Roxanne's claim." He said.

"You don't trust your sister?" I snickered.

"I don't trust that you didn't manipulate her."

Baxter re-cuffed my wrists behind my back and hauled me roughly to the holding cells. I was thrown into a cell next to Roxanne's. The clang of the metal door slamming was harsh to my ears. Roxanne came to the bars separating her cell from mine.

"Nico, are you okay?"

"I could be better." I joined her at the bars. "Why did you do that? I was trying to keep you out of this mess."

"Because I won't let my family haul the man I love away without a fight to prove he's innocent."

"You are incredible."

Roxanne smiled. "I know."

I sighed, resting my forehead on the bars. "I wish I could touch you."

Her brother threw me in here without removing the cuffs. Roxanne instructed me to turn around. Looking over my shoulder, I saw her crouched, using what looked to be a bobby pin to pick the lock on the handcuffs. After a few curses and a couple of minutes, my wrists were free. Roxanne beamed triumphantly. I cupped her face through the bars and kissed her awkwardly.

"Marry me."

"What?" She questioned, confused.

"Marry me." I repeated. "This isn't the romantic setting I was going to plan, but it doesn't change the fact that I want you to be my wife."

"This isn't a spur-of-the-moment question?"

"Nope." I grinned. "Paul is keeping the ring safe and secure, so you don't accidentally find it in my penthouse."

"Yes." Roxanne reached up to squash my face to the bars so she could kiss me. "I expect something more romantic when we get out of here."

"Come desideria il mio amore."

Twenty-Five

ROXANNE

Mom came to my rescue like a bat out of hell. She was fuming as Jaylen unlocked the jail cell. Though part of me wanted to run into her arms, I didn't want to leave Nico, so I stayed near our shared wall.

"Go." Nico urged. "You don't belong in here."

"Neither do you."

He cupped my cheek, his thumb brushing softly under my eye. "My innocence will be proven."

Yes, yes, it will be. I tilted my face into his hand and kissed his palm. Reluctantly, I stepped away. I rushed past Jaylen and went straight to my mom. She wrapped an arm over my shoulder and guided me out of the station.

"How did you know?" I asked softly.

"Jaylen called."

"He did?" I frowned.

"Yes, sweetheart, he did. He's a good man."

I didn't say anything. Just because Jaylen called my mom doesn't automatically put him in my good graces. With Nico behind bars, he could take advantage of the situation. I shook my head. Jaylen's not that kind of person. Yet I couldn't shake this feeling that he'd do anything to win back my affection.

"I'll drive you home." Mom said.

"No." I fished car keys from my purse, collected from an officer on my way out of the holding cells. "I don't want to leave my car behind."

"I can arrange to have your car taken to your apartment."

"I should check in with Lexi."

"Very well." Mom stopped me to pull me into a hug. "Don't worry about Nico too much. If he's innocent, the evidence will prove it."

"He is innocent." I declared. *Does she not believe that?*

"I'm sure he is." She appeased me.

"Mom." I stopped walking, took a deep breath, and continued. "I love him."

She cupped my face, searching for something in my eyes. "The evidence will prove his innocence."

"Nico asked me to marry him." I told her.

Her eyes widened in surprise. That wasn't exactly the reaction I was hoping for. I thought she'd be happier that someone I've been dating asked me to marry him.

"I said yes."

Mom hugged me tightly. "I'm happy for you, but your father won't be pleased."

"I know."

"Make sure you tell him sooner than later."

I bit my lip. "His reaction to me dating Nico wasn't stellar. If I tell him I'm Nico's fiancée, he may be blinded by hatred and keep Nico behind bars."

Mom pondered for a moment, reluctantly agreeing that it was possible. She suggested waiting until Nico was free before telling Dad. She gave me one more hug and congratulations before heading to her car. I got into mine and went to the salon. Lexi was far more excited about Nico popping the question. She asked me about a ring, which reminded me that Paul had it.

I drove to Nico's condo building and went to security. When I asked about the ring, Paul grinned and went to fetch it. He placed a dark blue velvet box on the desk. With trembling fingers, I reached for the small box, opening it slowly. A large pear-cut pale blue diamond blinked back at me. Small diamonds decorated the filigree sides. Taking the ring out of its velvet bed, I examined it closer. Nico had the inside of the ring engraved: Ti Amo Bella. It was perfect. I slipped it onto my finger, holding my hand up so the light would catch the diamond. I couldn't wipe the smile from my face. All I need now is my man by my side.

I spun the engagement ring around my finger as I stayed at the edges of Club Obsidian. Nico told me that he signed over ownership to the club when he wanted to open up the dealership. Yet, Tyler insists that Nico owns Obsidian. Only the current owner can prove that Nico's name is no longer associated with Obsidian. This is the only reason why I'm here. It's to collect proof of Nico's innocence.

I eyed the doorway near the bar. I'm assuming the bathrooms would be that way, and I'm also hoping there's a way to get to the office. With a glance up at a row of windows on the second floor, I watched a shadow pass by. The owner should be up there. I hope. With a deep breath to steel my resolve, I walked through the doorway. Clubgoers crowded around two doors marked as bathrooms. *This crowd can cover my sneaking.* Pushing through the crowd, I pretended to be one of the many waiting women for the bathroom before slipping through an employee-only door further down the hall.

I was immediately confronted with a set of stairs. Up I went, walking like I was meant to be there. Hitting the top, I looked in both directions. With a guess as to where the office was located, I started down the short hallway. *One of these doors is not like the others.* I singsong in my head. Stopping at a door near the end of the hall, I knocked. With no answer, I opened the door and popped my head in. I'd found the office.

"I could have sworn someone was here." I mumbled while slipping into the room.

I hesitated. I'm not sure if I should wait or if I should start searching myself. I approached the desk, still weighing the pros and cons in my head for both actions. A door to the left opened, and I spun to see Franco. My entire body tensed, and I regretted my decision to come to the club, but there was no turning back.

"Farfalla." Franco cooed, sounding pleased. "What a surprise."

"Franco." I replied coldly.

"What brings you to my office?" He began walking closer.

"You're the owner of Obsidian?" I pretended not to know.

"I am." He leaned against his desk casually, arms crossed over his chest and ankles crossed. "What can I do for you, Farfalla?"

I stood my ground, crossing my arms and lifting my chin defiantly. "Prove it."

He raised a brow. "Prove what?"

"That you're the owner."

Franco grinned. "Why would you need proof of my ownership of the club?"

I pursed my lips. I didn't think this through enough. If it was anyone else, I may have been able to explain. Seeing as it's Franco, I can't seem to bring myself to admit that it's for Nico. It almost feels like a betrayal. Franco doesn't need to know that Nico is behind bars. He studied me, his eyes roaming over my body, sending a shiver of disgust through me.

"I could be persuaded." Franco's grin widened.

"I'm not offering you a thing." I growled.

He shrugged, then went around the desk and took a seat. "Then I guess you don't want Nico out from behind bars that badly."

I couldn't hide my surprise. "How did you hear about that?"

"That's not important, Farfalla."

"If you know that your brother is in trouble, then you should know what it'll take to help him." I countered, trying to regain my footing with this man.

"The question is, do you know what it'll take to free your fiancée?"

I didn't comment on the fiancée part. He probably saw the ring and assumed. "What do you mean?"

Franco opened a bottom drawer in his desk. I leaned forward, catching a glimpse of what might have been a safe. His hand covered the buttons so that I couldn't see the combination. Franco rifled through the safe and then pulled out a folded piece of paper. He placed it on his desk, opened it, and showed me its contents. It was the ownership transfer papers that Nico had told me he'd signed.

"These will free my brother."

"Why didn't you submit those ownership papers to city hall?"

"Haven't I?" He raised a brow, taunting me.

I winced. "What do you want Franco?"

Franco opened a top drawer and pulled something out. "I want you for one night."

"No." I answered instinctively.

253

He ignored me and continued. "This Saturday is the mayor's charity auction. I want you to be my date for the evening."

I stared at the ticket he'd placed on the desk, then glared at Franco. "Why?"

"There are too many questions in that one word. You'll have to be more specific, Farfalla."

"Why me? Why not someone else? You Frangione men have the looks that'll make many women swoon." I cringed, not meaning to compliment him.

Franco smiled. "I need a respectable, beautiful woman on my arm for the night. Those other women you speak of that I could find on this short notice are not suited for a black-tie event like this."

"Why do you need a respectable woman for this?"

"I wish to make connections." He answered. "You can charm the wives while I talk to the husbands. You can play the role of girlfriend for the crowd."

Warning bells were going off in my mind. If Franco is the criminal Tyler should be looking for, then these connections will only aid him in his crimes. If I go with Franco, I can take the information I learn to my brother. *What will Dad think?* Mom and Dad will be going to this event, and they'll see me with Franco. Dad is already pissed about my connection to Nico. This will only push him over the edge.

"I need an answer, Farfalla."

I focused on the transfer papers. "Fine."

"Good." Franco sounded pleased, pushing the ticket forward. "To ensure you don't back out of this deal, I'm going to need collateral. How about that ring?"

I cradled my hand to my chest, covering it with my other hand. "No."

"You can't have the transfer papers for free."

"I'm not." I bit out. "I'm stuck going to the charity auction with you."

"If I hand you these papers now, what's stopping you from not going with me?" He countered.

"My word."

Franco shook his head. "That ring will guarantee your commitment."

In a way, he's right. Those papers are the only reason why I agreed to the charity auction. I stared down at the glittering ring Nico had to have custom-made just for me. *I am not giving this to Franco.* As much as I hate it, there is something else Franco can hold onto until Saturday.

"I'm keeping the ring." I declared, looking Franco straight in the eyes. "You can hold onto the transfer papers until Saturday."

There was a flash of surprise in Franco's expression, too quick to really notice if I wasn't paying attention. Franco put the papers back into the safe with a smile. He then stood, coming around the desk. My body tensed. The last time he'd gotten close, he'd kissed me. If I backed away, it'd only show him my fear, and I refuse to show any outward fear.

"I look forward to Saturday." Franco stated.

"The event starts at five, and I'll be here at four. You'll hand me the transfer papers, and then we can leave." I told him. "At the end of the event, you will bring me back here so I can drive myself home."

Franco reached out, cupping my cheek. "Let's seal it with a kiss."

I glared at him, inwardly proud that I didn't flinch from his touch. "Absolutely no—."

My refusal was cut off as Franco swiftly hauled me against him and sealed his lips over mine. I shoved at his chest, disgust rolling through me. A strangled sound escaped me. Franco loosened his hold on me, but not enough for me to break free. I shoved at his shoulders, trying to keep him as far away from me as possible since he wouldn't let me go.

"This is not how a girlfriend should act, Farfalla."

"I'm not your girlfriend." I sneered. "So don't kiss me."

"But for the night, you will be. How many couples do you know that don't kiss?" He asked, amused.

"I'm your date only." I told him. "Kissing is forbidden. You break that rule, and I will make a scene."

Franco frowned. "What other rules are you going to give me?"

"I don't know yet." I admitted. "If you do something I don't like, I'll let you know. If you do it again."

"You'll make a scene." Franco finished while taking a step back. "By the end of the night, your opinion of me will soften, Farfalla."

"You keep calling me that. What does it mean?"

"Butterfly."

Twenty-Six

NICO

I woke up stiffly. The cot in the cell is too uncomfortable to get a good night's sleep. I need a shower, a change of clothes, and a coffee. Luxuries I won't get. *Maybe I can get a coffee.* I tried to see if there was an officer down the hall, but I couldn't get a good angle from my cell. I stretched my muscles, trying to relieve the kinks before sitting down on the cot. I don't know how long I'll be stuck in these cells, and I am wondering if I should call my lawyer. I winced at the thought. My lawyer is my father's lawyer. If I call, then my father will be tipped off that I'm in trouble.

I heard the sound of a door opening and closing. The sound of voices could be heard from down the hall, but I couldn't clearly hear what was being said. All I could distinguish was that one was male and one was female. Very soon, footsteps came down the hall.

"Nico." Roxanne exclaimed, rushing to get to my cell.

"Bella, what are you doing here?"

"Getting you a coffee before I go to work." She carefully slipped the to-go cup between the bars. "Did you get any sleep?"

"A little. The cot's not too comfy." I took a sip of coffee. "Thank you for this."

"I'll be back later today."

"You shouldn't have to see me like this." I wanted her in my arms.

Roxanne wrapped her hand around the bars. "You shouldn't even be here."

I took her hand, smiling at the ring on her finger. "You went to Paul."

"I did."

"Ti amo, Bella." I kissed the ring.

"Ti amo." Roxanne tightened her fingers in mine. "Saturday. I'll have proof of your innocence on Saturday."

I frowned. "Bella, what did you do?"

She pulled away. "I have to get to work. I'll be back later."

"Bella!"

I called after her, but she didn't turn around or return to explain. *What did she do? What proof is she talking about?* Not knowing twisted my gut. Taking another sip of coffee, I scowled at the cup. I need Roxanne to explain her cryptic parting. It's only going to bother me for the rest of the day.

True to her word, Roxanne returned. She looked nervous.

"I brought you soup."

She held up a thermos with a timid smile. Roxanne looked to the officer who followed her. He grunted, took the thermos, unlocked my cell and shoved the thermos at me. Then he slammed the metal cage shut with a loud bang before locking it again. Roxanne flinched at the sound.

"Keep it short." The officer ordered before retreating down the hall.

"How was your day?" She cringed at the question. "I mean, are you being treated fairly? Did you have anything to eat? I brought you soup."

"Yes." I lifted the thermos. "Thank you."

Roxanne flushed. "You shouldn't be in here."

No, I shouldn't be. I sighed, reaching through the bars to cup her face. "I'll be out before you know it."

Roxanne looked up at me. There was something in her eyes that worried me. Something more than determination to see me free. I opened the thermos and poured a cup of soup, choosing to return to this subject a little later. The warmth of the vegetable soup warmed my insides. All I had today was a ham sandwich and a bottle of water, both probably from a vending machine.

"How was your day?" I turned the question on her.

"I spent the morning with my lawyer and at city hall. Lexi is officially a partner in Dagger Designs." She beamed. "We have an appointment this week with my realtor to look at a few properties for a second location."

"That's amazing, Bella."

"I wanted Lexi to be my partner since day one, but she insisted she only wanted to be a receptionist and my helper. I'm glad she finally accepted my offer."

"Bella, this morning you said you were going to have proof of my innocence Saturday. What is that proof?"

I broached the subject while she was in a favourable mood. Her shoulders stiffened, and her smile faded.

"I need to know." I pressed.

She took a step back and averted her gaze. "I asked the current owner of Obsidian for the transfer papers. They prove you don't own the club."

My blood ran cold, fear and anger gripping me. Who knows what Franco would have asked from her just for those papers. He's shown an interest in her, so it can't be good. I didn't know Franco had never submitted the transfer of ownership papers until yesterday. Because he didn't submit them, I can only suspect that he always intended to use me as a scapegoat for his crimes. Separating myself from my family was supposed to protect me, even just a little. I may never get out of here.

I put the thermos down. "What did that cost you, Bella?"

"One evening." She wrapped her arms around herself. "I'm to be his date at the mayor's charity auction this Saturday."

"No."

"Nico." Roxanne looked at me.

"No." I said more firmly, slamming my fist against the bars. "Franco is too dangerous. Agreeing to this means he can get you to agree to anything else."

"He'll give me the papers when I show up for the night." She explained, stepping forward again. "I can negotiate with your brother. Originally, he wanted my ring as collateral, but I couldn't give him that. I bargained for the papers instead."

"You should have never gone to Franco in the first place."

"I want you free." She reached through the bars to cup my face. "I want to prove that my brother is wrong."

"Bella." I said softly, trying to tap down the anger and fear.

"If our situation were reversed, you'd do anything for me." Roxanne countered.

I pulled her hands from my face to kiss her palms. Holding them to my chest with one hand, I reached through the bars to cup her cheek. She tilted her face into my touch. With all seriousness, I answered her.

"I would burn the world down until you were at my side again."

"See?" Roxanne beamed. "You're the dragon who'd burn the world for me. All I did was make a deal with the devil."

Franco isn't the devil. My father is. I wasn't about to correct Roxanne. I don't need her coming up with the idea that a deal with my father will have faster results than a deal with Franco.

"I don't trust Franco." I told her. "He's scheming something."

"I don't trust him either."

"Then don't do this." I begged uselessly. "Maybe you can convince your brother to raid the club. He'll find the papers himself."

"It won't work." She shook her head.

"Why not?"

Roxanne's gaze flickered down the hall where the officer ventured earlier. She bit her lip, not saying anything more. She didn't have to. I understood. My brother, or maybe it's my father, would have officers in their pocket. They'd be paid well to tip off a Frangione about a police raid. I know that, but how would she? Did Franco give something away? He's too calculating to do that.

"It's okay, Bella." I pulled her in for a kiss. "Don't let your guard down around Franco."

"I won't." She kissed me again. "Besides, I have a fiancée who'll burn the world for me."

I smiled. "I'm not worthy of you."

"You are worthy."

"Ti sei il mio sole." I kissed her palms again.

"Rox." Detective Parry's voice broke through our little bubble. "Let me take you home."

"I'm perfectly capable of getting home myself." Roxanne countered bitterly, glancing at him. "I drove here myself and everything."

"Bella, let him escort you."

Roxanne looked at me, then grunted her acceptance. Parry looked at me questioningly but didn't voice anything. With an extended hand to the hall, he gestured for Roxanne to leave. She gripped my face to kiss me before stepping back. I watched her disappear with Parry.

I went back to the now chilled soup. There is no way Roxanne should be going to the charity unprotected. I want to be the one watching her back, but I might have to settle with it being her ex-lover. The only way to get him to help me is to tell him where Franco took the undercover cop. I could take a guess, but if I'm wrong, it could jeopardize Roxanne's safety.

I stood, about to call down to the officer on duty when Detective Baxter came into view. He looked paler than when I saw him earlier today. *Something must have happened.* He stared at me as if he was trying to figure out why the last puzzle piece didn't fit into the puzzle.

"Where is my officer?" Baxter questioned, his tone monotone and tired.

"I don't know."

"Why did you tell my sister to be escorted home?"

I looked beyond Baxter, not sure who could be listening. I leaned into the bars, lowering my voice. "Not here."

Baxter studied me. His jaw tightened, and he pulled out his handcuffs. I extended my wrists for him to handcuff me, then stepped back. Baxter unlocked my cell, grabbed my arm and hauled me away. He didn't take me to an interview room this time. Instead, he took me to what appeared to be an unused office. He sat me down roughly in a chair next to a desk, closed the door, and then took the other chair.

"Talk." Baxter ordered.

"Roxanne may be in danger." I told him. "Having her escorted is the best I can do to protect her in my current situation."

"What kind of danger?"

"Unpredictable."

Baxter ran a hand through his hair and leaned back. "Using my sister is low, Frangione."

"What happened between this morning and now?" I questioned cautiously.

"Your men sent a video."

My spine straightened. "What kind of video?"

Baxter eyed me, a debate going on in his mind. When he made his decision, he pulled out his phone to show me the video. The missing officer was tied to a chair, bloodied and bruised. There was a sign around his neck that read pig, and the man didn't look like he was moving. Background noise was a mix of indistinguishable things. Someone came into view, shook the officer's shoulder, and when he didn't move, was punched in the gut. The officer curled inward at the attack and groaned. The man was still alive, barely. Snickering could be heard, probably from the cameraman.

"Play it again." I requested. "Keep the sound off."

Baxter scowled at me but played the video again. This time, I focused on the surroundings. The officer wouldn't have much time left. I suspect Franco wanted this video made for a reason. For what reason, I'll never know. I don't want to know how my brother's mind works. The camera moves slightly when the officer gets punched, so he stays in full view, and that's when I see it. I snatched the phone, hit pause and brought my face closer to the screen. When the officer curls in on himself, I'm able to see what's behind him. *I know where this was filmed.*

"You need to add more security to the mayor's charity auction this Saturday." I told Baxter while handing his phone back.

"Why would I do that?" He scowled.

"To keep Roxanne safe."

"I need a better reason than that." He cringed. "I need proof of danger."

"Then let me go. You can tag along to keep an eye on me."

Baxter laughed. "That is definitely not happening."

I pointed to the phone. "Get me a map, and I'll show you where that was filmed. I suggest you get it yourself, discreetly."

"Why?" Baxter narrowed his eyes suspiciously.

I pursed my lips. Telling him what I'm about to say could get me killed. I will do anything if it means Roxanne will be a little safer. Roxanne is my top priority.

"I don't know who." I started. "But officers are working for my father and brother."

Baxter's eyes widened like this was news to him. I could see the wheels turning as he revisited past events. Events I'm sure involved failed attempts to arrest anyone in my family. Suddenly, Baxter stood and left the room. He came back a few minutes later with a coffee. Baxter handed me the drink, then from behind him, a folded-up map.

He opened it on the empty desk. "Where is my officer?"

I stood, eyes searching over the streets of Frostham. I set the cup down to point at a spot. "This is where your grandfather was shot, and this is where the video was filmed."

"Are you certain?"

"About 90% certain." I admitted. "I can not guarantee the officer will still be there."

"Why are you suddenly so talkative?"

"Franco is making a move." I gritted my teeth. "I don't know what his end game is, but it somehow involves Roxanne."

"My sister?" Baxter reeled from that tidbit.

"I will do anything to protect her. I love her."

Twenty-Seven

ROXANNE

I'VE BEEN DREADING THIS night all week — the mayor's charity auction. Businesses across Frostham put items in for the auction, such as gift cards, spa weekends, and dining experiences, and all the money from the auction goes toward a charity or two. This year, it is the food bank.

I strung my engagement ring on a long chain and placed it around my neck. Nico will remain near my heart all night while I play the role pleasant date for Franco. I double-checked my appearance before heading out. Franco had to have informed his bouncer of my arrival because when I banged on Obsidian's front door, the man let me in before I could tell him who I was. I made my way to Franco's office.

"Farfalla." Franco looked up from doing paperwork when I arrived. "You look stunning."

"Thank you." I mumbled. "Where are the papers?"

"Safe."

"I want them." I held out my hand.

"And you'll have them after the auction." He stood and tugged on the shirt cuff, pulling it past the jacket's arm length.

"No. You agreed. You'll hand me the papers when I arrive, and then we'll leave for the auction."

"Did I?" Franco's lips twitched upward. "I don't recall."

I narrowed my eyes at him and crossed my arms. "You sealed it with a stolen kiss."

He stepped around the desk. "Remind me."

I stepped back, went to a chair and sat down. "No transfer of ownership papers, no date."

"Girlfriend." He corrected sternly.

"Date." I leaned back, getting comfortable. "There will be people at this auction who know me, and I don't want to give them the wrong idea. How will it look if I show up to this auction as your girlfriend and then become Nico's wife shortly after?"

Franco frowned. His nostrils flared, and his eyes darkened. He clearly didn't like me arguing. My shoulders stiffened, afraid he might break off the deal. Franco closed his eyes and took a deep breath.

"Don't worry, Franco, I'll still play nice." I said softly, grimacing. "But I'm not going anywhere without those papers."

"Fine." He growled.

Going back around his desk, he pulled the papers out of the safe and handed them to me. Relief relaxed my nerves as I folded them and placed them in my clutch. Standing, I walked with Franco out the back door of the club and down the alley to a waiting car. He opened the back door for me and then slid in next to me. Somehow, I'll get these papers to my dad tonight. Franco placed a hand on my knee, his grip a clear warning for me not to pull away.

The mayor's auction has always been opulent. Invitees included officials in the city and the elite. This year it's held at Frostham's art museum. Franco offered me a hand getting out of the car, then wrapped it in the crook of his arm. Paparazzi took pictures of the attendees going up the steps to the museum. I plastered a smile on my face to uphold my end of the deal with Franco.

I noticed all the cops keeping paparazzi at bay and the metal detectors as we walked into the museum. *They must have received a threat.* Security wasn't this tight last year. After going through security, we were directed to the European Art wing. The auction was held in the main hall, the doorways leading to specific art styles such as Renaissance, Gothic, and Romanticism, each guarded to ensure no one wandered off.

People mingled while waiters walked around with trays of hors d'oeuvres and champagne. Franco plucked two glasses from a passing waiter, handing one to me. He then wrapped an arm around my waist, fingers digging into my hips to keep me close as he mingled. I was surprised by how many of the wealthy elite knew Franco. I tried to focus on the conversations he had, but the wives and girlfriends insisted on stealing my attention. I'll never be able to provide Tyler with any information if I'm unable to listen in.

The attending officials, such as judges and lawyers, avoided Franco. I could feel their judging looks as they looked our way. I kept my eyes open for my mom and dad, but there were so many people at the auction that I couldn't find them in the crowd. Franco steered me around the room to people he wanted to talk to. The mayor saw me. With a smile, he came straight to us, blocking Franco from going to whoever was next on his list.

"Roxanne!" The mayor exclaimed, holding out his arms to me.

"Mayor Jones." I stepped out of Franco's hold.

"Arnie, please." He pulled me into a hug. "How's business?"

"Booming."

"That's good." Arnie looked past me. "Is this your boyfriend?"

"No." I shook my head. "This is Franco Frangione. He brought me along as his date for the evening."

"Good, good."

He let me go, and Franco pulled me back into him. I did what I could to keep some distance between our bodies, but he wouldn't have it. Franco tried to start a conversation, but the mayor ignored him and focused on me.

"My son is back from his tour overseas." Arnie said proudly. "You and your family should come by next Saturday for a BBQ. I'm sure Simon would love to see you."

"I'll pass that along." I told him.

"Here you are, Arnie." Janet, his wife, handed him a glass with amber liquid. "Roxanne, you look stunning."

"Thank you, Janet." I eyed the drink in Arnie's hand. "Where did you get that?"

"At the bar." She pointed in a general direction behind her.

I turned to Franco. "Would you like anything?"

"Whisky." His smile was tight. "Neat."

Janet pulled me out of Franco's arms. Hooking her arm in mine, she led me to the bar. I leaned into her, thankful for the escape.

"That's not your fiancée, is it?" Janet questioned in a hushed tone.

I looked at her, startled. "Not in any lifetime."

"Good." She nodded her approval. "Your mom told me you got engaged but didn't tell me with whom."

"You may want to tell Arnie that I'm engaged. I think he just tried to set me up with Simon."

Janet laughed. "You know, Simon has had a crush on you since you two were in high school."

"Really?" I conjured up an image from the last time I saw him. "I didn't know that. Why didn't he say anything?"

"You both went in different directions, him off to the army, you off to college. Then you got that boyfriend. Simon was disappointed, but when you broke up, he didn't think it was the right time to make a move. Right when he was ready, he got called away."

Janet paused when we reached the bar so I could order — a whisky for Franco and a wine for myself. A familiar presence came up behind me. I turned to see Nico. He looked delicious in his suit.

"Nico!" I wrapped my arms around his neck and kissed him. "What are you doing here?"

"I made a deal with your brother." He settled his hands on my hips. "I hate seeing Franco's hands on you."

"I hate his hands being on me." I scowled.

"Come with me." He urged. "We can slip out of this place without him noticing."

"And go on the run? Not happening." I cupped his cheek and shook my head. "Think of the consequences."

"You're right." Nico reached past me, grabbing the drinks I'd requested. "I'll be watching, Bella."

He pecked my lips, handed me the drinks, then slipped into the crowd. Knowing Nico was here, watching my back, gave me a sense of calm. If Franco does anything, then Nico will swoop in to save me.

"Who was that?" Janet gave a low whistle.

"My fiancée." I stated proudly.

"He's good-looking."

"He's more than that." We stepped away from the bar, and I jutted out my hip. "In my clutch are some papers. Can you get them to my brother or dad? Tonight. Without Franco knowing?"

"Sure." Janet frowned while fishing for the papers. "I don't know where either of them are right now."

"He'll be here, somewhere."

She tucked the papers in her clutch. An announcement was made that the auction will begin shortly. I left Janet to find Franco, who ended up finding me. He wrapped his arms around me and guided me to the front half of the hall, where everyone had gathered. The area was blocked by a curtain when we arrived earlier this evening. It has now been removed to reveal tables set up for dinner. We found our names on a board and made our way to our assigned table. At the place setting was an auction paddle. While we ate, we could buy the items up for bid.

I didn't buy anything. Franco purchased a package for a romantic night out. I glared at him, hoping he didn't expect me to be his plus one for that package. Dagger Designs put in a gift card for a complete set of nails. I was surprised by how high the bidding went. It made me giddy to know just how much the women of Frostham want to have their nails done at my salon. I'll have to enter something next year, too.

It was another couple of hours before Franco decided it was time to go. The moment the car parked in front of Obsidian, I slid out, needing to get away from Franco.

"Good night Farfalla." Franco drew me in to kiss my cheek. "Drive safe."

I glared at him, not sure if those words were a veiled threat or not. Getting in my car, I put my engagement ring on my finger before driving off. It felt weird not to wear the ring, even if it's only been a few days since I've been engaged. Now that it's on my finger, everything feels right.

Twenty-Eight

NICO

I GOT LUCKY. THE undercover cop was found at the warehouse, beaten, bloodied, and bruised. From the whispers I heard when I was put back in my cell, the officer's life was hanging by a thread but alive. If Baxter didn't get him to the hospital when he did, then a funeral would have been planned.

A day after I told Baxter about the warehouse, Jaylen Parry came to get me. He placed the handcuffs on my wrists too tightly and roughly jostled me out of my cell to the same office Baxter took me to last time. With a hand on my shoulder, he pushed me down into a chair. Both Baxter's entered the room, father and son.

"Frangione." Captain Baxter growled. "I'm willing to offer you a deal."

I raised my brow, curious as to where this was heading. Whatever the deal is, he's reluctant to provide it. All I can hope is that this deal involves protecting Roxanne.

"A reduced sentence if you help us to tear down your family's underground empire."

"What exactly are you charging me with?" I questioned.

"Obstruction of justice for withholding important information that would have saved an officer of the law."

"I heard whispers that you got to the officer on time." I stated.

The Captain's jaw tightened. "Barely."

"I'm also innocent of all other crimes you think I've committed."

"The evidence says otherwise."

"What evidence?" I countered, annoyed. "If all you have is my name on a piece of paper, then you have nothing."

Jaylen's hand tightened on my shoulder, and Captain Baxter's face turned red. *I'd hit the nail on the head.* They really have nothing on me, which means this whole thing has been a charade to get my cooperation. Roxanne was put through this pain because of them. I sat back, not feeling very cooperative at the moment. I'd figured out their game but found no enjoyment in it.

"We'll add more security to the mayor's charity auction." Baxter added.

"I want all charges dropped." I locked eyes with Roxanne's brother. He's the only sensible one in the room.

"Can't do that."

"Then I can't help you."

"Rat bastard." Captain Baxter grumbled. 'You're just like your father."

Anger surged in me so fast I couldn't control my outburst. "I am nothing like him."

I barely registered the hands on my arms that held me back from the Captain. I wanted nothing more than to punch him for such a comment. Tyler had stepped between me and his father. He shoved at my chest, urging me back.

"You said you'd do anything to protect Roxanne." Baxter said. "Prove it."

At the mention of Roxanne's name, the anger cleared. She wouldn't be happy if I punched her father. I know because she's already asked me not to punch her brother. I'll have to prove to him that I'm nothing like my family. He's so convinced that all Frangiones are the same it'll be a difficult task.

"Here's my counteroffer." I spoke directly to the younger Baxter. "You let me go to the charity event Saturday to keep an eye on Roxanne. If I'm right and something happens to her, then I want all charges dropped."

"If you're wrong?"

"I won't fight for my innocence. You'll be able to charge me however you wish."

Baxter scoffed at that. "How about you become a C.I. if you're wrong?"

A criminal informant? I thought about it. If my family learns I'm a C.I., they could kill me. If something happens to Roxanne, I'll burn the world down, whether for revenge or to find her, and I'll start with my father's underground empire. By becoming a C.I., I may be able to prove myself to Captain Baxter, for Roxanne's sake.

"Deal."

I held out my hand, and Baxter shook it. He gestured with his head to get me out of the room. Parry hauled me to my feet. Instead of taking me back to my cell, he took me back home. After removing the handcuffs, I immediately went for a shower. It felt good to get the grime of the past few days off of me. Refreshed and in new clothes, I ventured to the kitchen.

"You don't deserve Rox." Parry growled.

"No, no, I don't." I agreed, opening the fridge in search of food.

"Then you agree that you should let her go."

"I've tried." I pulled out the Chinese food I had earlier in the week when Roxanne spent the night with Lexi. "She wouldn't go. Roxanne chose me, so I'm going to keep her."

Parry was my guard until Saturday night. At the charity auction, I was handed off to Baxter. We kept to the edges of the crowd, keeping an eye on the guests. I was searching for Roxanne.

"Here." Baxter handed me a folded piece of paper. "This is the deal we discussed."

I read over the details. It's exactly as we discussed, though a little more elegantly written than what was verbalized. It's been signed by a judge, an attorney, and Captain Baxter. All it needs is my signature. *This is perfect.* I took the offered pen and signed the papers.

On instinct, I looked up. "Bella."

She looked stunning in an emerald green dress. It showed off her curves while still being modest. The top exposed only one shoulder and arm, keeping her mostly covered from neck to feet. She held a silver clutch and around her waist — Franco's arm. I shoved the deal at Baxter but kept the pen tightly in my hand. I'll stab Franco first in the hand for touching her, then the eyes for looking at her.

"Don't." Baxter gripped my shoulder. "If your brother realizes you're here, he'll probably realize you made a deal with us. I don't want to put my sister in any more danger."

"Let me talk to her."

"Not now." He wrangled the pen from my hand. "Find a time when she's not anywhere near Franco."

"Fine." I gritted my teeth.

Baxter kept me close, and I kept a close eye on Roxanne. Her smile was forced as Franco took her around the gallery. Despite his arm around her waist, Roxanne tried to keep a distance between them. Eventually, the mayor made his way over to them. He seemed to know her, pulling her away for a hug.

Franco drew her back into him the moment he let go. His wife then showed up, taking Roxanne away.

"Go now." Baxter nudged me. "Make it quick."

Roxanne beamed when I came up behind her at the bar. She immediately wrapped her arms around my neck and kissed me. The tension in my body eased with her in my arms.

"I made a deal with your brother." I told her after she asked what I was doing here. "I hate seeing Franco's hands on you."

"I hate his hands being on me." She scowled adorably.

"Come with me." I urged, desperate to take her away. "We can slip out of this place without him noticing."

"And go on the run? Not happening." Roxanne cupped my cheek and shook her head. "Think of the consequences."

"You're right." I reached past Roxanne for the drinks she requested. "I'll be watching, Bella."

I stole another kiss, handed her the drinks, and then slipped back into the crowd. When I returned to Baxter's side, an announcement was made about the auction starting. Baxter kept us at the back and out of sight. Franco bought a package for a romantic night out. I knew Franco only bought that for one reason — to use it on Roxanne. He thinks I'm in jail, which gives him clear passage to my woman. Our father still wants to use her. I'll be damned if they get to her before I get her to the altar.

They stuck around for another couple of hours before they left. I had to watch my fiancée leave the event with my brother. Baxter kept me from following. He said he had someone assigned to follow Roxanne home. We stuck around for another half hour until Baxter received a call that Roxanne had left Obsidian unharmed. We slid into his car so he could take me home.

"10-50." The radio in Baxter's car crackled. "10-50."

Baxter got on the radio asking for more information. He received a street name and was told that an ambulance was on its way. He turned on the lights and raced to the scene.

"What does 10-50 mean?" I asked.

"Motor vehicle accident."

"Why the rush?"

Baxter glanced at me. "The car is in the direction of Roxanne's apartment."

I felt sick. "You don't think it's her?"

"I hope not."

Lights flashed at the scene from other cop cars and an ambulance. Baxter had to park a couple of cars back. We got out of his car and rushed to get closer to the scene. A single vehicle sat on the side of the road, the side smashed in, and the driver's side door flung open. The air bag had deployed, saving the driver's life.

My heart sank when I recognized the car. "Bella!"

I rushed to the car, but she wasn't there. I could only stare at the empty spot. There was blood on the airbag, thankfully not enough to indicate she was seriously harmed. Turning to the nearest paramedic, I grabbed him by the uniform.

"Where is the driver?"

"I don't know." He said, trying to detach my fingers from him. "There was no one there when we arrived."

"Let him go." Baxter separated us. "First on the scene said this is how they found the car."

"This is Roxanne's car." I told him pointlessly. "Your sister's car."

"I know that, but she's not here."

"Then where is she?"

I already knew the answer, but I didn't want to hear it. Hearing it would make it accurate.

"Taken." Baxter said. "I'll make sure there's an A.P.P. out."

"Franco. He has her." I said, knowing it's the truth.

"There's no proof."

My eyes fell back to the car. Franco has something to do with this. He has my woman. Where and why, I don't know. I approached the vehicle, hoping a clue was left for me to follow. Nothing physical. He's too careful for that. I leaned in. *Cazzo.* There's a subtle scent of cigars. I know one person close to Franco and my father who smokes those awful things.

"We'll find Roxanne." Baxter promised. "I won't stop searching until she's home."

"Our deal is still valid?"

"Yes."

"Good." I turned to Roxanne's brother.

"What are you going to do, Nico?"

"Bring my fiancée home."

Franco is a dead man. The moment I have Roxanne safely back in my arms, I'm going to gut him. No one will take her from me again. I will burn my father's empire to the ground.

Glossary

CRISTO: CHRIST

Fottermi: Fuck me (curse)

Peccato: Too bad

Ma davvero non voglio: But, I really want to

Grazie per questo: Thank you for this

Voglio vedere: I want to see

Scopami: Fuck me (sexual)

Per favore: Please

Bella: Beautiful, also a term of endearment

Cristo donna: Christ woman

Come si desidera: As you wish

Buona notte: Good night

Che cazzo fai: What the fuck are you doing

Spiegare: Explain

È altamente qualificato: He's highly qualified

Cazzo: Fuck

Bastardo: Barstard

Sorprendente: Amazing

È Perfetto: It's perfect

Grazie: Thank you

Lei è perfectta: She is perfect

Angelo: Angel

Fermare: Stop

Farfalla: Butterfly

Non era mia intenzione ferirti: It wasn't my intention to hurt you

Ti sei il mio sole: You are my sunshine

Cazzo sì: Fuck yeah

Bellissima: Beautiful

Sei la donna più bell ache abbia mai posato gli occhi: You are the most beautiful woman I've ever laid eyes on

Sei sicuro: Are you sure

Lavoro eccellente: Excellent work

Il mio raggio di sole: My ray of sunshine

Come desideria, amore mio: As you wish, my love

Buongiorno amore mio: Good morning my love

Ti amo: I love you

Ti sei il mio sole: You are my sunshine

About the Author

Ivy Marie grew up an army brat. Moving every two or three years, and finally settling in Ottawa, Ontario, Canada. When she's not writing she's at work, or spending time with her friends.

Both friends and family are supportive of her creative expression. She's found comfort in Supernatural Romance, with werewolves and vampires as the main creatures she writes about, and also in Contemporary Romance.

Ivy Marie writes for her own enjoyment. She also hopes that the joy she feels while writing is expressed and passed on to you.

Connect

I really appreciate you reading my book! Here are my social media coordinates;

Facebook: www.facebook.com/IvysStolenHearts
Instagram: ivymariebooks
Blue Sky: @ivymarie-author.bsky.social
X: @IvyMarie_Books
Website: www.ivymarieauthor.com

Don't forget about my wonderful cover artist – Shawna Russ;

Instagram: shawncolourart

Also By

Keep an eye out other books by Ivy Marie.

Contemporary Romance
Thief in Paris
Bad Decisions (Book 1 of Decisions Duet)
Late Decisions (Book 2 of Decisions Duet)
Surprised by Love ~ Coming 2025
Fan the Flames ~ Coming 2026

Paranormal Romance
Stolen Heart
His Hunter
Bound to the Reaper (Book 1 of Reaper)

Reaper Undercover (Book 2 of Reaper) ~ Coming 2026

Reaper Forever (Book 3 of Reaper) ~ Coming 2027

Witch Troubles ~ Coming 2025

Like Hell series (Paranormal Romance) ~ Coming 2028

Like Hell Mario (Prequel)

Like Hell this is Real (Book 1)

Like Hell this is Normal (Book 2)

Like Hell this is Happening (Book 3)

Like Hell Alternative (Alternate Reality)